She smiled w
hand.

'Can we start ag
staff nurse here,
and amicable working relationship.'

He reached out and took her hand in his. 'And I'm Matthew Carvalho, medical registrar, and if you promise not to bite my head off, every time we meet. . .' His voice trailed away and before Jane could realise his intention he'd brought her hand to his mouth and gently kissed the back.

Dear Reader

This month we touch upon personal grief for the heroines in TROUBLED HEARTS by Christine Adams, and SUNLIGHT AND SHADOW by Frances Crowne, both handled with sensitivity. PARTNERS IN PRIDE by Drusilla Douglas and A TESTING TIME (set in Australia) by Meredith Webber give us heroines who are trying hard to make a fresh start in life, not always an easy thing to do — we think you'll both laugh and cry.

The Editor

Christine Adams is a registered nurse living in the West Country, who has worked for many years in the National Health Service and still nurses part-time. She has been writing for the past ten years, mainly short stories and articles. She finds the dramas and tensions in the medical world an ideal background in which to find plots and storylines.

Recent titles by the same author:

LOVE BLOOMS
DEMPSEY'S DILEMMA

TROUBLED HEARTS

BY
CHRISTINE ADAMS

MILLS & BOON LIMITED
ETON HOUSE, 18–24 PARADISE ROAD
RICHMOND, SURREY, TW9 1SR

First published in Great Britain 1994
by Mills & Boon Limited

© Christine Adams 1994

Australian copyright 1994   Philippine copyright 1994
This edition 1994

ISBN 0 263 78602 1

Set in 10½ on 12 pt Linotron Times
03-9406-50092

Typeset in Great Britain by Centracet, Cambridge
Made and printed in Great Britain

CHAPTER ONE

'IF YOU don't let go of my arm right now,' Jane snapped, 'I'm going to. . .' Her empty threat faded into the air, for there was nothing that she could do. She hoped that the man looming over her couldn't hear the tremor in her voice. It was unlikely he heard a word of what she was saying above the persistent shrieking of the car alarm. But whether or not her voice was audible, it was obvious he didn't intend to release her until he himself was ready. Taking a deep breath, Jane suddenly jerked her arm and, to her surprise, managed to get free.

'I'm telling you again, I didn't do anything to your precious car.'

With a muttered curse, the man pulled keys from the pocket of his expensive-looking car-coat and pressed a small switch, bringing a blessed quiet to the hospital car park. Jane swallowed, her moment's relief gone, her green eyes widening in apprehension. From her five feet two the man seemed enormous, and his grip on her arm had been vice-like.

There was a silence that lasted for several seconds as he stared at her from heavily lashed eyes, eyes that looked almost navy in the dull light of the March morning.

Jane shivered; she wasn't sure why. Perhaps it was the overwhelming maleness of the man, a strong masculinity unfamiliar to her, brought up as she had

been in a female household with only mother and
older sister since her father's death.

'I've told you,' she repeated, 'I wasn't doing
anything, anything at all.'

'In that case, why did the alarm go off?'

Impatiently, Jane pulled her woollen hat more
firmly over her ears. 'I don't know. If you'd only
listen for a moment, instead of jumping to conclusions. I couldn't get to my car because yours is
parked so inconsiderately, it's blocking mine in.' She
gestured angrily towards her battered Mini, which to
her fevered imagination looked almost as cowed as
she herself felt.

The breadth of his shoulders seemed to fill the
narrow space between the two vehicles and Jane
waited with barely concealed impatience for him to
move out of the way. Not for anything did she intend
to actually push past him. There was a look in the
depths of his dark eyes that she didn't trust and an
almost imperceptible lift at the corner of his wide
sensual mouth, that hinted. . .he couldn't be laughing at her, surely?

'If I made a mistake, I'm sorry.' His voice was
deep, with the merest trace of—hesitation? accent?
She wasn't sure which.

'If you made a mistake. . .' Jane exploded, her
normally fair skin flushed with annoyance.

'If I made a mistake, I apologise, but you must
admit that there has been a spate of thefts from cars
throughout the hospital grounds, and when I saw
you standing there. . .' He shrugged, and the offhand gesture infuriated Jane as none of his previous
actions had done.

Ostentatiously she rubbed at her arm, the sleeve of her dark grey suit sliding back and revealing a painfully thin wrist. 'Well, are you going to stand there all day?' she said sharply, her tone all the fiercer to hide her nervousness.

Impatiently the man brushed back his thick dark hair, hair that had been tumbled out of place by the force of the wind. Suddenly he grinned and the smile transformed his face, etching tiny creases at the corners of his eyes and revealing a groove at one side of his mouth.

Defiantly she stared back at him for a moment, before manoeuvring herself through the tiny space between the man's dark blue BMW and her own Mini. In the narrow gap, she was forced to brush against an unexpectedly powerful chest, and a drift of expensive cologne, in keeping with the almost imperceptible aura of wealth about the man, reached her nostrils.

Hoping that her expression wouldn't betray her embarrassment, Jane decided there was no way she could confess that she had in fact been responsible for the alarm. How could she have known that her irate thumps on the roof of the BMW would set up such a racket and bring its owner hurrying to her side?

'There is no way I can open my car door with you standing there.' Gazing straight ahead, her face was in line with the top of his coat. She could hear her breath rasp in her throat and wondered again why she should feel so on edge.

Not answering, the man gestured to the sign above them, the words 'Staff Car Park' plainly visible in

the streak of watery sunshine that chose that
moment to break through the clouds.

'So?' Jane raised her eyebrows, her sea-green eyes
flashing angrily.

'You don't mean to tell me that you're a member
of staff?'

'As of my interview this morning,' Jane said
sharply.

He drew in his breath with a small hiss of surprise.

'Did I pass you in the corridor? I thought there
was something familiar. . .' His voice trailed away
as he studied her more closely. Caught in the force
of the man's stare, Jane fidgeted with the front of
her coat, unable to suppress a shiver that had
nothing to do with the cold March wind whistling
directly from the Cotswolds as it cut between the
old-fashioned red brick buildings of St Adhelm's
hospital.

'You don't look old enough to be at work,' he
began, shaking his head in obvious disbelief, then
with a shrug he unlocked his car door and carefully
slid into the front seat.

'I'm twenty-four years old. Just because I'm only
five feet and a bit,' Jane muttered huffily. But the
stranger in the expensive-looking coat ignored her
protest as he switched on the ignition and edged
forward. With a whirr of an electric motor he
lowered his window.

'I'm giving you the benefit of the doubt this time,
but I should warn you I don't take kindly to anyone
tampering with my car.' Without a backward glance,
he put the car in gear, the engine purring gently as

he moved towards the tarmac drive leading to the hospital gates.

Eyes flashing, Jane drove behind him, wincing at the grating noise her engine made in contrast to that of the BMW.

'What a pig,' she muttered, pulling out around a cyclist who was fighting against the blustery wind; she went through the hospital gates and headed towards home. 'All that fuss over a car. Wonder who he was?' She pushed a tape into place in the stereo and tapped out the rhythm on the steering-wheel as the music blared into sudden life.

Gradually her annoyance drifted away and a slow smile crossed her face as she thought over her recent contretemps. Somehow the altercation with the man she'd met had lifted some of her depression. It was surprising, she thought, how a little blast of temper could get the adrenalin flowing. Pity he'd been so objectionable; she'd always had a weakness for dark-fringed eyes.

'Anyway, enough of him,' she told herself, moving steadily along Brodleigh High Street, before pulling up to allow a lorry to back into a covered entrance next to the shopping precinct. Gripping the steering-wheel tightly, Jane closed her eyes for a moment. How long would it take before she was able to see a lorry without feeling sick? she wondered. She grimaced as a sharp stab of pain pierced through her, making her bend towards the dashboard.

'Oh, Penny, why did you and David have to take that corner at that particular moment?' Jane brushed her eyes with the back of her hand and sniffed loudly.

Even though she'd not been there, she had such a
vivid mental image of the accident, the articulated
lorry jack-knifing across the road, the car crushed
without warning. The horrors of one short moment
had had such catastrophic results on their little
family.

Now, her niece and nephew were orphans, and
she and her mother, as well as coping with their loss,
had to face a completely disrupted lifestyle: extra
responsibility for her mother, despite the arthritis
that affected her so badly. And Jane herself had
thrown aside all her plans, the ITU course in London
that she'd been looking forward to, the flat she'd
arranged to share with friends. Still, she couldn't
succumb to her own feelings of grief, for there were
Emma and baby Harry to consider from now on.

For a moment, she forgot her anguish and stared
objectively at her hand, noticing as if for the first
time how badly her watch now fitted. God, she
hadn't realised just how much weight she'd lost since
the funeral. She certainly couldn't afford to get any
thinner or there'd be nothing left of her.

An angry toot from the car behind made Jane jerk
in her seat and she hurriedly shifted into first gear
and moved along the road which narrowed abruptly
as she passed the cathedral, its clock tower square
and solid above the Cotswold stone buildings of the
surrounding shops. Just a small rise to the dual
carriageway and then she would be home.

'It's me, Mum.' Jane shut the front door behind her,
throwing her keys as usual into the patterned china
dish that sat on the hallstand just inside. An appetis-

ing aroma drifted from the kitchen as she went through to the room at the back of the small house she now shared with her mother.

'Shut the door, love; don't want the smell of cooking to drift throughout the house.' Mrs Shelby glanced up from the stove, and paused from stirring at a large saucepan on its top to wipe her hands in the striped apron that protected her jumper and skirt.

'Sit down, Mum, I'll see to that.'

'Jane, I may have arthritis, but I'm still capable of pushing a spoon round,' her mother countered sharply. 'You take the weight off your feet and tell me how you got on this morning.' Eyes a softer greeny-grey than Jane's studied her and with a sigh Jane perched on one of the wooden chairs by the big old table, now set with a blue checked cloth. Thankfully, she pushed off the unaccustomed high-heeled shoes.

'I got the job, start next week as staff nurse on nights on Coronary Care.'

'Oh, Jane, well done.' Her mother's face darkened momentarily. 'Though it's a terrible shame you've got to miss out on the course. You were really looking forward to that, weren't you?'

'Honest, Mum, I don't mind at all, and night duty is the best plan for the time being; it means I can be here with you when the children need attention and when I'm working they'll be in bed asleep. Hopefully we can work things out so that there won't be too much for you to do.'

'You'll have to sleep during the day; it won't help any of us if you crack up.'

'I'd rather be busy and I shan't do anything silly.
That spaghetti sauce smells divine. I didn't realise
how hungry I was.' Abruptly Jane changed the
subject. It was such a difficult time for both her
mother and herself, not least in that Jane had to be
so careful not to give the impression that her mother
was an added burden. After all, it wasn't Muriel
Shelby's fault that she was limited in what she could
do.

'It's almost ready.' Mrs Shelby's voice broke into
Jane's thoughts. 'Get the plates from the cupboard,
will you, Jane, and cut a few slices of bread?'

'You get the bread, I'll strain the spaghetti.'

'Jane,' her mother said warningly.

'All right.' Jane grimaced an apology and moved
quickly to the cupboard. Soon, they were sitting at
the table, the spaghetti and sauce on their plates
disappearing rapidly as both ate hungrily.

'I'm glad to see you've got your appetite back,'
Mrs Shelby nodded in approval as Jane wiped up the
last of the meat sauce with a piece of bread then sat
back with a satisfied sigh.

'That was great. I must admit, it's the first
time. . .' Jane paused and listened intently. 'I
thought I heard something — yes, I did, young Harry
demanding attention.'

Hurrying upstairs, she went along the small landing to the back bedroom. Harry's tentative cry of a
few moments ago had developed into a full-scale
roar by the time she reached him. Red-faced, he was
standing in his cot, gripping the bars so tightly that
every chubby finger was dimpled.

'Hey, hey, what's all that noise about,' Jane

murmured softly; as she lifted him his cries ceased
immediately, the occasional hiccup the only sign of
his annoyance as Jane wiped his face and changed
his nappy, before pulling an all-in-one suit over his
struggling limbs.

'Come on, down we go.' Hoisting him to her
shoulder, Jane returned to the kitchen.

'I think he wants something to eat.' She strapped
her nephew into his high chair and handed him a
spoon, wincing as he started to bang on the tray in
front of him. 'You just stack the dishes, Mum, I'll
wash up later,' she continued, spooning meat and
vegetables from the small dish of food into Harry's
gaping mouth. There was a blissful quiet as the nine-
month-old baby swallowed as avidly as a young bird.

'Do you think he realises?' Jane asked the question that had haunted her waking thoughts and
dreams since the death of her sister. How much did
Harry understand? Did he realise his parents weren't
there? In some ways it was easier for Jane to deal
with his three-year-old sister, for Emma was able to
say something of how she felt. But with Harry. . .
Jane sighed.

'We can't know what he thinks,' Mrs Shelby
answered softly. Ignoring her daughter's request,
she had already washed their few dishes and was
busily wiping down the draining-board. 'All we can
do is make sure that both Harry and Emma know
how much they're still loved, even if they've only
got their granny and auntie to look after them now.'

'You're right, Mum, I must try not to get too
morbid.'

'It's understandable.' Mrs Shelby sat on the small

wooden bench beside Jane. 'Now, while Harry is spreading his Marmite fingers all over the high chair, tell me everything about the interview this morning.' Her mother looked hard at her. 'I must say you've got a lot more colour in your cheeks today.'

'That's probably the result of losing my temper. There was this man in the car park—well, talk about overbearing. You should have heard the way he carried on.' Eyes sparkling, Jane regaled her mother with the details of her encounter after her interview. Her voice rose in annoyance as she once more remembered the way the man had behaved, and she didn't notice the small smile that crossed her mother's face.

'Well, with a bit of luck you won't see him again.' Her mother laughed as Jane paused for breath. 'It's very interesting, of course, but I was hoping to hear about the interview itself.'

'Of course, sorry. I got carried away there, didn't I? Well, there's not much to tell except that I got the job and start next week.' Jane took her mother's hand and gently rubbed the swollen joints with her fingers. 'Are you sure you'll be able to manage the children while I'm sleeping? I know Emma will be at nursery during the day but. . .'

'Jane, I've told you. Stop worrying. If you can cope with working nights, I can surely manage to take care of Harry for a few hours at a time. Don't forget, they're my grandchildren. I want to do my share. I know,' Mrs Shelby said hastily as Jane started to speak. 'You like to do everything yourself, but in these circumstances, you will have to let me contribute what I can.'

'Well, at least I'll be in the house, even if I'm sleeping, so you can always call me if there's an emergency.' Jane smiled with an assurance she was far from feeling. She ran her fingers through her short fair hair, her eyes darkening with the thought of all that lay ahead.

'Anyway, enough of that. What's next on the agenda?' Getting to her feet, she put Harry's dish in the sink, wrung out a flannel and wiped his face and hands. 'You go through to the sitting-room and I'll get the kettle on for a cup of tea.' She glanced at the blue enamel clock on the small oak dresser. 'We've got another hour before I need to fetch Emma from the nursery.'

Ushering her mother from the kitchen, Jane soon had the tea brewed, a tray set with cups and saucers and carried it through to the living-room.

'All right,' she called in answer to Harry's squeal of annoyance at being left in his chair. 'I'm coming back to fetch you, never fear.'

Loving his baby smell and the feel of his velvety skin as she hugged him close, Jane pushed aside all thoughts of the family's problems. She would manage. She'd always coped with things in the past and there was no reason to suppose that she wouldn't be able to do so in the future.

Though money would be tight until the details of David's insurances were sorted out, with what she earned on nights and her mother's pension, small though it was, they would be fine.

Setting Harry in his playpen in the corner of the living-room, Jane sank down beside her mother on the settee and took a cup of tea from the tray.

'Golly, I'm weary. I think it was all the emotional stress of the interview this morning.'

'Just put your head back, have a bit of a nap when you've finished your tea. Harry is more than happy and I'm well occupied, struggling with this cross-word.' Her mother held the folded newspaper in the air.

'Perhaps I will, get my strength up before I collect Emma.' Jane squeezed her mother's arm, leaned her head back and closed her eyes. But, weary though she was, sleep eluded her.

Little prickles of annoyance kept her mind buzzing as she remembered the man in the car park and the offhand way he'd behaved.

Forget him, she told herself sharply. With any luck, it was a once-in-a-lifetime meeting. He wasn't worth fretting over, nor his precious car. But it was a pity he'd been so objectionable. A half-smile curled her mouth as she remembered his dark-fringed eyes; it was very rarely that one saw eyes that colour, such a dark blue they appeared almost black.

At least her interview had gone well and Barbara Mellor, the medical nurse manager, had been really helpful. It was a shame that Jane'd had to postpone her course, but at least night duty would mean she'd be able to spend more time at home. And in Coronary Care it would give Jane some insight into acute nursing, something that she'd been out of touch with since her training days.

It had been interesting, if a little daunting, to look round the unit, with the monitors flashing steadily, the central console, the defibrillator used to regulate abnormal heart rhythms, the small side-room where electronic pacers were fitted, the little artificial 'black boxes' that provided regular impulses for hearts that beat too slowly.

'How do patients manage with those when they hurry? Does the pacemaker automatically increase its rate as the normal heart would?'

'Good question.' Sister had smiled at Jane. 'There are pacemakers in the pipeline which will in fact do that. But the present ones in use stay at a fixed beat, so patients with them have to get used to maintaining a steady rate of activity.' Jane's green eyes danced at the memory, pleased that she'd been enough on the ball to think of such a thing. It showed that six months in female orthopaedics hadn't stopped her being observant in a different branch of nursing.

'I know I'll be able to cope with night duty,' Jane had reassured her interviewer, straightening her grey skirt, which like the rest of her clothes was too large now for her slender figure.

New job, completely new lifestyle with extra responsibilites, avoiding dark blue BMWs with dark-eyed owners. . . She smiled to herself, then gradually the warmth of the room and the gentle background noise of Harry playing happily with his bricks slipped away and soon Jane forgot everything and drifted into a light doze.

CHAPTER TWO

'Now you're sure you'll be all right?' Picking up her bag, Jane turned anxiously from the doorway between the living-room and hall and looked back at her mother once more.

She wasn't surprised that she felt so unwilling to leave the cosy scene in front of her. The flickering flames of the gas fire lit the back wall, the television glowed in the corner and Mrs Shelby looked settled for the evening in her big armchair, where the rust-coloured fabric matched the main shade of the carpet and set off the bright sunshine-yellow cushions in its depths.

'Of course I'll be all right. You're the one I feel sorry for, having to turn out on a night like this.' Jane's mother gestured towards the curtained windows where the sound of the wind whistled with an almost vicious strength, occasionally rattling tree branches in the garden and bringing a shiver despite the warmth of the room.

'Don't worry, I shan't be out in it for long; it only takes about fifteen minutes to get to the hospital.' Jane smiled bravely. 'I'm quite looking forward to starting work, to tell you the truth.'

'Well, you look and smell very nice. That's that new Dior perfume you were keen on trying, isn't it?' Mrs Shelby sniffed appreciatively.

Jane nodded. 'My small treat for my first night.'

With a wave, she hurried to the front door and stepped out into the night. Clouds scudding across the sky threw fitful shadows so that the moonlight streaked the front path with patches of silver, giving their small garden an unfamiliar, almost eerie appearance. Even the few bushes seemed threatening as they tossed and rustled alongside and Jane was glad to get into her car and slam the door.

'Not the most pleasant night to have to go out,' she murmured as she switched on the ignition and pulled away from the kerb. Since her sister's accident she'd been apprehensive at times when driving, but the car responded sweetly, its newly serviced engine smooth in the night air. Gradually Jane's nervousness faded and soon she'd left her road and pulled into the more brightly lit dual carriageway.

It's strange to be going to work when every one else is either going out or settled at home, she thought, as she moved up through the gears and set off along a surprisingly empty highway. By the time she'd reached the cathedral and passed the edge of the main shopping precinct, the wind had died down and Jane approached the hospital, thankful that at least she would be able to park more easily at night, probably close to the main entrance.

She couldn't help a grin as she remembered her meeting with the irascible BMW owner. At least she hadn't got to worry about his car this evening.

The door to the main corridor squeaked noisily as she went inside and she winced at the echoes raised by her new duty shoes. She'd have to get rubber heels fitted as soon as possible. She'd forgotten how much noise leather ones made, especially at night.

'I've put Sally Chalmers with you tonight.' Miss Benson, the senior night sister, smiled encouragingly as Jane signed in at the office. 'She's had a lot of experience in Coronary Care. Don't bother to come to the office in future, go straight to Ward Ten.' Her grey hair brushed back from her face, her rather square features unsmiling, Miss Benson looked very intimidating, but Jane could sense the warmth behind the rather stern expression and smiled back gratefully as she picked up her three staff nurse uniforms and set off along the corridor to the main lift.

Thank goodness there'd be someone who knew the routine, to guide her through her first night. She tried to remember the last time she'd worked in CCU as the lift carried her swiftly to the first floor. It must have been during her training and that was at least three years before. Things were sure to have changed a lot since then.

The lift hissed gently to a stop and the doors slid back but as Jane stepped out her dresses slipped from her arms. Trying not to panic, for the doors were already closing, Jane scrabbled feverishly at them and sighed thankfully when a large capable hand reached down and whisked her uniforms from the floor.

'That could have caused problems, if they'd jammed in the doors.' The voice was familiar, though the man spoke much more quietly than when she'd last heard it. Jane's heart sank. What was he doing here? Of course, he'd been parked in the staff car park, so almost certainly worked at the hospital. Keeping her head forward as she muttered her

thanks, Jane quickly took the dresses and walked to
the ward entrance, her shoulders hunched about her
ears. Perhaps if she kept her face turned right away,
he wouldn't recognise her. After all with his height,
he could probably see only the top of her head
anyway.

She breathed a sigh of relief as she heard him turn
in the opposite direction. In the nurses' changing-
room, it took her only minutes to slip off her jeans
and sweatshirt, pull on one of her dark blue uniform
dresses and pick up a plastic apron from the rack in
the corner of the room. Why on earth had she had
her hair cut so short? she thought, frantically brushing at it with impatient fingers. It was fine with her
own clothes but definitely didn't seem right at work.

'Thank goodness we don't wear caps any more,'
she muttered, pulling a face at her reflection and
walking nervously into the ward and to the nurses'
station for report.

Sally, a pleasant girl with flyaway dark hair, was
already perched on one of the chairs. Her long-
legged height immediately made Jane feel smaller
than ever. But her friendly smile and the day sister's
welcome put Jane at her ease and she gradually
relaxed as she scribbled all the relevant details in a
small notebook, placing it in her pocket once Sister
had finished.

'I think if you stay close to me, at least for the
time being, I'll show you where everything is and
give you some idea of the routine. You can do more
on your own when the workload gets quieter as the
night goes on.'

Moving swiftly on her long legs, Sally led Jane to

the six-bedded unit, the beds all separated by screens or gaily flowered curtains.

'Dr Carvalho takes care of all the patients, particularly any night emergencies, although officially we have two consultants on call here,' Sally explained.

'Good evening,' she called as heads swivelled towards the two nurses. Jane had a blurred impression of white sheets, rumpled duvets and faces staring back at them, all different but with a common denominator of suffering or apprehension written on each one.

'Dr Carvalho is actually our medical registrar; he's on duty tonight, so you'll get a chance to meet him. Good evening,' Sally repeated to each patient as they went from bed to bed. 'This is our new staff nurse — she's learning the ropes tonight, so just all of you behave yourselves.'

Jane nodded and smiled, overwhelmed by the fast-changing images, trying hard to absorb the sights, sounds and smells of her new work area. Her most vivid impression was of quiet, so different from the noisy bustle of a general ward and she found herself tiptoeing in Sally's wake, trying hard not to click her heels too noisily on the floor's polished surface.

'I've done very little time in CCU.' Jane bit her lip apologetically. 'Nothing really since my training.'

'Not to worry, you'll soon get the hang of it.' Sally flung back a series of doors. 'There's the sluice, linen cupboard, treatment-room and that one at the end is the store cupboard. We share a coffee-room. . . Oh, good evening, Dr Carvalho.' Sally glanced over

Jane's shoulder. 'Didn't hear you arrive. Let me introduce you to Jane Shelby, our new staff nurse on nights. You'll probably be seeing quite a lot of her, for you do seem to attract all the night emergencies, don't you?'

Jane spun on her heel then stopped, the half-smile wiped from her face as she recognised the man staring back at her, his white coat open to show the collar of a dark blue shirt and loosely knotted light-coloured tie, which to her apprehensive stare gave him an almost gangster-like appearance.

'Dr Carvalho and I have already met,' Jane muttered, wondering what malign fate had thrust her into close working proximity with a man she'd already decided she never wanted to see again. She winced as her hand was seized in a strong grip and vigorously shaken.

'Have you? That's good.' Sally raised finely pencilled eyebrows. 'I'll leave you to chat a minute, while I go and see about getting the night drugs organised.' She turned to Jane. 'Come to the central desk when you're ready. That's nice, isn't it? Someone you already know, working here. Will help you to feel much more at home.'

'So you've come to work in Coronary Care?' He gazed at her, and Jane could sense a flicker of amusement in his voice. Embarrassment made her abrupt.

'Yes, I have.'

'You have no need to be nervous.'

'I'm not nervous. . .well I suppose I am really.' Jane pushed impatient fingers through her hair. 'But you don't have to worry. . . Dr Carvalho, isn't it?

I'll make sure that I keep my car well away from yours.' She glanced up, really looking at him for the first time and knew she was right; there was a definite trace of laughter in the curve of that mouth.

'What's so funny about me?'

Hastily his expression changed, his dark eyes blinking in astonishment at her tone.

'I don't find you the least bit amusing,' he said stiffly. 'I was about to suggest we let bygones be bygones. I'm willing to forget the incident in the car park if you are, but I think it could be difficult for us to get on, especially if you snap at me like that.'

Jane drew in a deep breath, striving for control. It wasn't like her to behave in such a touchy manner. Dr Carvalho had probably been trying to put her at her ease, make her feel welcome. But there was something about him that made her defensive, as though he didn't take her seriously and it was aggravating to feel like that, particularly as she was on edge. But this time she was in the wrong, she had to admit it.

'I'm sorry,' she sighed, ruefully shaking her head. 'There's no justification for me to carry on in that way.' She smiled warily and held out her hand. 'Can we start again? I'm Jane Shelby, a new staff nurse here, as Sally explained, and I hope we'll have a long and amicable working relationship.'

He reached out and took her hand in his. 'And I'm Matthew Carvalho, medical registrar, and if you promise not to bite my head off every time we meet. . .' His voice trailed away and before Jane could realise his intention he'd brought her hand to his mouth and gently kissed the back.

Hastily she snatched it free. 'What do you think you're doing?' Her voice was sharp, for she was shocked, not at his action, flamboyant though it had been, but at the sensation that had travelled through her, a sensation that set every nerve-end tingling.

'I must go,' she said breathlessly. 'Sally will think I've absconded on my first night.'

Hurriedly she made her way towards the nurses' station, guided by the sound of Sally's voice.

'There you are.' The other nurse was already on her way round with drugs on a trolley, the patients' treatment cards at one end, a selection of syringes and medicine glasses at the other.

'We number the beds from one to six, starting at the door and working in a clockwise direction.' Sally pointed to the cubicles. 'If you would check this frusemide, forty milligrams for Mr Grant, then give the digoxin to the lady in bed four, we'll have the drugs finished in no time.'

Jane picked up the two tiny brown ampoules and carefully checked the dosage on each, putting them into a small tray beside the syringe.

'I hope Mr Grant has a urinary catheter,' she grimaced sympathetically, 'or he'll be wanting to use the bottle all night after that much frusemide.'

'We don't usually give the diuretics this late in the day.' Carefully Sally snapped off the necks of the two small vials and drew the liquid into a syringe. 'But he's got ventricular failure and needs to get rid of the fluid from his lungs.'

To Jane's relief, the patients seemed a cheerful group, and as she shook the tablets into the medicine

containers and passed them round, she found she
enjoyed the backchat and teasing which brought a
glow to her cheeks. Soon she was giving as good as
she got.

By the time she and Sally had finished the drugs,
tidied the beds, putting clean sheets on two where
the patients had been perspiring very heavily and
done a repeat electrocardiogram, it was nearly
eleven o'clock and Jane was feeling more relaxed,
much more than she'd expected.

She was relieved that Matthew Carvalho—
unusual name, she mused—had disappeared and
she was able to concentrate on her work. It was hard
enough to try and absorb the routine of the unit
without having the very disturbing presence of the
doctor hovering somewhere in the background.

'Come on. Coffee. I'll switch on the percolator
and would you collect up the report charts and put
them on the desk? Can you file Mr Tomkins' new
ECG in his notes as well?'

'Of course. And while we have our coffee, would
you mind explaining exactly what the ECG shows? I
don't really know what I'm supposed to be looking
for.' Jane frowned at the zig-zag patterns on the blue
graph paper as she put it tidily in place.

'Here you are.' Sally soon reappeared with a tray
set with coffee jug and pretty flowered mugs and put
it on the corner of the desk.

'Ground coffee.' Jane sipped hers appreciatively.
'What luxury.' She delved into her bag. 'I've got
some chocolate biscuits here. To celebrate my first
night, so to speak.'

'Great.' Sally's eyes lit up. 'Though I shouldn't,'

she continued mournfully, 'as I'm trying desperately to lose weight. How do you keep so slim?' She stared enviously at Jane's slender frame.

'I'm not usually as skinny as this. But I've had a few problems lately and it made the weight fall off.'

'Lucky you,' Sally muttered through a mouthful of crumbs. 'If I'm upset, I just seem to put it on.'

'Well, it's just as well we're — ' Jane began.

'Aha, I thought I could smell coffee.' The voice cut in unexpectedly, making Jane nearly spill her drink as Matthew appeared from the furthest cubicle.

'Dr Carvalho, how long have you been there? We could have been saying all sorts about you, and think how embarrassing that would have been.'

Matthew grinned as Sally got to her feet and fetched another mug, returning to fill it for him.

'Milk and sugar?'

'No, thanks.' He shook his head. 'Black for me.'

Jane sat not speaking, hugging her coffee mug in her hands, staring quietly down the length of the unit. There was something intimidating about Matthew Carvalho, and even though they'd agreed to start afresh in getting to know one another, she, the perpetual chatterbox, found herself suddenly tongue-tied now he was near.

Luckily, Sally wasn't affected in the same way. Her voice rose and fell in the background, providing a soft accompaniment to Jane's thoughts.

'Where did you two meet? You didn't say.' The question burst into Jane's reverie and she straightened apologetically in her seat.

'Pardon? Were you talking to me?'

'Who else could I mean?' Sally gestured at the now silent unit.

'Well,' Jane shrugged, 'it wasn't anything exciting. We were merely parked near one another in the hospital car park the other day.'

'What Jane is too polite to say is that I lost my temper because I thought she'd been tampering with my car.'

'Oh, well, it doesn't matter now, does it?' Jane muttered hastily, feeling the warmth flow through her. She wished Matthew wouldn't study her so intently. In the dim light from the lamp on the desk, it was difficult to read his expression, but whatever his thoughts, his concentrated gaze made her feel very uncomfortable.

'You were going to explain the ECG to me.' Seizing the folder, Jane pulled out the relevant sheet of paper and passed it across to Sally.

'There's no need for me to tell you about it as long as Dr Carvalho is here. He can explain it much more clearly than I can.'

Before Jane could say a word, Matthew had shuffled his chair next to hers and they were side by side, both gazing at the ECG reading. He glanced sideways at her from under strong dark brows.

'Have you seen the demonstration sheet with all the different cardiac abnormalities?'

Jane shook her head.

'Well, we'd better go through those as well. First of all, you need to be able to recognise normal heart rhythms. If you know exactly what they look like, obviously you'll be able to recognise any abnormalities much more quickly.'

'Well, I think I can just about recognise whether a reading is normal or abnormal.' Jane perched on the edge of her chair as Matthew unpinned a large sheet of paper from the noticeboard beside the desk and slid it out in front of them.

'Here you are.' He leant forward, his finger tracing the lines on the chart. 'This is the base line. As you know, the heart contracts and pumps blood to the lungs for oxygenisation.' He glanced up and smiled. 'Sorry to be so basic. I'm not talking down to you, am I?'

'No, not at all.' She tried desperately to relax, but was uncomfortably aware of the pressure of his shoulder so close to hers and of the sheer masculinity that seemed to radiate from him. She stared enthralled for a moment at the curved shadow on his cheek from thick dark lashes that any girl would envy. Hurriedly she forced her thoughts back to the sheet of paper as he carried on speaking.

'The signal for these contractions is the spread of electric currents through the heart muscle. What an ECG does is record the electric currents, and it can tell us when something is wrong, either with the currents themselves or with the responses because of damage to the muscle.'

'Um — had I better go and make sure Mr Jennings is all right?' Jane had a sudden desire to move away from the desk and the feel of Matthew so close to her.

'You don't have to worry,' Sally reassured her. 'They've all got their bells handy and if they need anything, they'll ring soon enough.'

Grudgingly, Jane sank back on to her chair. She

felt nervous enough at starting her new post; it wasn't going to make it any easier if she became twitchy every time Matthew was near.

Deliberately, she edged her chair away, pretending not to notice his questioning look.

But he continued to explain and soon she was absorbed in what he was saying, forgetful of how self-conscious she'd been earlier.

'Here we have Mr Jennings' cardiograph with the thrombosis that damaged the heart muscle. Can you see how the peaks on that line there are different?'

Jane bent forward and studied the chart more closely. 'I think so,' she muttered doubtfully.

'Tell you what,' he glanced at his watch, 'I have to go to X-Ray in a minute. You look at these during the night and the next time you're working I'll go over them with you to see exactly which ones you don't understand. Is that all right?'

He grinned disarmingly as he stood up.

Jane nodded hesitantly. 'Fine by me, but I should explain that I may be a bit slow picking it up. I was telling Sally that except for the odd relief day I haven't worked in Coronary Care since my training.'

'No problem; if you're keen enough, you'll learn. Any questions about what you've seen so far?'

'Not about the ECGs, but it seems to me you could get to be so busy watching the monitors or looking at these recordings, there's a danger of forgetting that they concern sick people. Technicalities being more important than the actual care, in other words.'

'Ooh, that's a bit nasty.' Matthew winced dramatically and leaned his hands on the desk. 'I wouldn't want you to get the idea that we forget what we're here for, and that is the patient. But in an acute area such as this, if you understand exactly what can go wrong and if the monitors give you warning in good time, which they should do, then your care will be that much more efficient, surely?'

'If you say so.' Jane laughed softly, suddenly more reassured than threatened by him.

There was silence for a few minutes as they each finished their coffee. Jane read the notes avidly and soon they were no longer an excuse not to talk to Matthew, but were of interest in their own right.

'God, I can't believe how much I've forgotten since my training.' Jane sat back in her chair, her eyes wide. 'It makes you realise what a fantastic piece of engineering the heart is and just how much can go wrong!' She grimaced at Sally. 'Now I'd better get that monitor you asked for just now. No, don't get up, it'll be good practice for me to find it myself.' She hurried to the equipment-room and stared along the top shelf. Ah, just where she'd remembered seeing it. She balanced precariously on a small step-ladder and struggled with the unexpectedly heavy piece of equipment. Busy concentrating, she didn't hear Matthew's approach.

'What do you think you're doing?' she gasped, red-faced with embarrassment as his hands seized her and he swung her easily to the ground.

'You should be more careful, you could easily have fallen,' he said abruptly, but the warmth in his eyes belied the sharpness of his words.

'I was fine,' she said crisply, aware of the rapid beating of her heart at the feel of his strong hands at her waist, praying that he wouldn't be able to sense it as well. 'You didn't have to interfere; I'm no damsel in distress.'

'You've certainly made that obvious.' The smile immediately left his face. 'I just happen to think that there's no shame in occasionally asking for help. I can reach the top shelf much more easily than you, so why shouldn't I do it?' He shook his head in disbelief and said no more, but the stiffness in his shoulders as he took the monitor and left her conveyed very clearly how he felt.

Pulling her uniform dress straight, Jane hurried after him, aware that she might have given offence but unable to think of how to apologise. Thank goodness, Sally seemed oblivious of any awkwardness between them.

'Thanks. If you put it on the trolley just there, I'll set it up in a minute by the empty bed. I didn't get a chance to ask you before, Jane, but where have you been working up till now?'

'Female Orthopaedic which, as you know, consists very largely of care of the elderly these days. All those fractured necks of femur.' Jane pointed to the paper on the desk. 'Certainly I'll have to put my brain cells to work on this little lot.'

'I think that the more you learn the more you realise how little you know, if you see what I mean.' Leaning across the desk, Matthew replaced his cup on the tray. 'I've certainly discovered that since I've been doing my research.'

'What are you researching exactly?' Eager to make amends for her earlier rebuff, Jane smiled shyly at him as he leaned against the corner of a cupboard by the desk. In the dim light, his eyes were unreadable, deep, dark shadows outlined in olive skin. The flash of white teeth as he smiled lightened the almost threatening look that for a moment held Jane's gaze despite her wish to tear her eyes away.

'I'm looking into. . .' Beep. The noise abruptly cut off Matthew's words. 'Blast!' He pulled the small pager from his pocket and studied the numbers on the digital display. 'X-Ray calling me. I shall have to go. It's been nice talking to you. Thanks for the coffee.' He grinned and hurried from the ward, the hem of his white coat flying out behind him.

Jane stared after his disappearing back. 'He's a bit overwhelming, isn't he? Still, I think he means to be kind.' She leant back and stretched her feet out in front of her.

'I was quite surprised when you said you'd had words, I must admit.' Sally rested her elbows on the desk. 'He's always been very pleasant and helpful here and he never gets nasty if you have to call him out in the night.'

'Where's he from? He doesn't sound English at times.'

'I believe he's part Portuguese, hence the unusual surname, Carvalho. You seem very interested,' Sally said slyly.

'It's nothing like that. It's just that I don't want to blot my copy-book with him in the future; after such a disastrous start I feel I must be a bit careful.'

'Oh, he'll have forgotten all about that business in the car park, if that's what you're worrying about. He's not one to carry a grudge. Now are there any questions about what goes on or are you quite happy so far?'

The night passed surprisingly quickly and Jane was relieved at how soon she settled into the routine. It was very different from places she'd worked in before, but when it was quiet, she studied the charts and patients' folders with interest, determined to make a good impression the next time she saw Matthew.

She couldn't help feeling disappointed that he didn't visit the ward again, but, despite her efforts, thoughts of him returned to keep her company anyway. At far too frequent intervals. She didn't know what it was about him that had made such a strong impression on her but certainly, there was no way she could push him from the forefront of her mind.

'Come on.' Sally hauled Jane to her feet as soon as they'd given their report to the day staff. 'Time to go home.'

Jane sighed and ran her fingers through her hair. It still felt strange, the short, stubby haircut almost prickling at her fingers.

'See you tonight.' Jane waved and walked briskly to her car, enjoying the feel of the fresh air on her skin and the bright spring sunshine that gradually lit up the morning sky. There had been no worried phone calls from her mother, so hopefully everything had gone as well at home as it had for her first night on duty.

With a feeling of *déjà-vu*, she paused as she reached

the car park and saw the large dark blue BMW neatly parked alongside her Mini.

It had to be some kind of joke; it was difficult to believe it had been completely accidental. Jane stared all around but there was no sign of the BMW's owner. Suddenly overcome with nerves, she scurried to her own car, unlocked the door and pulled away as swiftly as she could.

As she made her way past the cathedral and turned towards the dual carriageway, she wondered that her heart should be beating so fast. Surely she wasn't scared of Matthew Carvalho? Perhaps not, but she'd made very sure that she hadn't touched his precious car as she'd left the hospital. Humming with the relief of getting away without mishap and also at the thought of a successful night's work completed, Jane drove steadily home. And for the first time since the loss of her sister, the future didn't seem so totally black. In fact, her voice was almost light-hearted as she drew up outside the house and went in to greet her mother and the two children in the kitchen.

CHAPTER THREE

'WELL, maybe the new routine has upset Emma at times, but Harry's been no problem at all.' Mrs Selby refilled their teacups and handed one to Jane.

'Thanks, Mum. I must admit I was worried when she seemed so tearful the first couple of days at the nursery, but this morning she was fine. Really keen to be with her new friends. And they've got marvellous facilities and staff there, even though the building itself is a bit old-fashioned.'

'Harry's slept for a couple of hours most days and with the lovely spring weather——' Jane's mother continued, pointing to where the kitchen door stood wide, afternoon sunshine spilling across the step and lighting up the rather gloomy corner near the old-fashioned larder. The occasional scent from the garden drifted in to mingle with the smell of hot toast. 'With the lovely spring weather, I've been able to take him to the park each afternoon.'

Jane's three nights of duty had passed quickly and she was relieved at how well she'd managed to sleep during the day. Though sometimes she felt disorientated at getting up in the middle of the afternoon, such as now. She glanced at her mother.

'Your hands don't seem to be causing you too much pain, despite the extra work,' she observed hopefully. 'And they're definitely less swollen.'

'They're nothing to worry about.' Muriel Shelby smiled across the kitchen table.

'I've settled in much more quickly than I thought I would.' Jane added an extra spoonful of sugar to her tea and stirred busily. It was funny, she thought, this craving for sweetness that she had when she first got up after her day's sleep.

'How about the other nurses on the ward?'

'They seem a friendly lot. I shall be sorry not to be working with Sally next week, but in future we could easily be on different shifts. No, Harry, don't do that.' Wrapping her dressing-gown tightly around her middle, Jane reached across to the high chair and seized a plastic brick that was rapidly disappearing into Harry's gaping mouth.

He sent up a momentary squawk of protest, but soon found something else to take his attention and Jane sat back.

'We will have to make sure you don't get so bogged down with all these extra responsibilities that you have no life of your own.' Mrs Shelby frowned as she stared at the tea that formed a miniature whirlpool on the surface of her cup.

'Mum, I don't need a social life at the moment. It'll take several months for both of us to come to terms with losing Penny and David. I'm sure that by the time we feel like going out again, everything will be sorted and as we want.' Jane seized her mother's hand. 'I reckon we're doing very well so far and neither of the children is suffering, which has to be our first consideration.' She stirred lazily at her tea.

'I think I'm going to enjoy working in Coronary Care, though it does seem odd having so few patients, especially after my time on that medical ward. It's not nearly as tiring, physically, for we don't have the lifting we had there. Do you remember how my back used to ache sometimes? Getting all my old ladies out of bed and into their chairs, helping the physiotherapists to walk them round the ward, turning them in bed, helping them with their meals. . . It makes the last three nights seem like a rest cure!' She hunched her shoulders and rolled her head from side to side, then glanced at the old-fashioned blue metal clock on the pine dresser.

'Oh, my God!'

'What's the matter?'

'Look at the time! I must fetch Emma.' Seizing clean clothes from the corner of the ironing board, Jane ran up the narrow flight of stairs to her room, hastily dressed in jeans and T-shirt and returned to the hall, picking up her keys on the way.

'I'll have to take the car, Mum,' she shouted, shutting the front door behind her. The nursery was only two streets away, and normally Jane enjoyed the short walk. But she couldn't risk being late, letting Emma think that she'd been forsaken; it would be ironic after her brave words of a few minutes before.

'Come on,' Jane muttered through gritted teeth, turning the key in the ignition. But the engine whirred like some wheezy asthmatic, belches of exhaust fumes filling the air with an acrid smell as the engine spluttered in protest.

'Oh, no, just when I'm a bit late. And I only had you serviced last week.' Banging the steering-wheel in frustration, Jane scrambled from the car and

shrugged her arms into her anorak. Slamming the
door behind her, she half walked, half ran up the
steep incline towards the nursery.

Don't start fretting, Emma, she thought, her face
twisting anxiously at the possibility of the little girl's
distress.

By the time she'd reached the big iron gate that
fronted the rambling Victorian building, Jane had to
pause, nursing a painful stitch in her side.

The sound of the car horn, a deep resonant parp,
made her swing round.

'Oh, no, not you,' she muttered, catching sight of
the BMW at the edge of the kerb and conscious that
her quieting pulse had picked up speed again.

'Are you ill?' Matthew Carvalho leapt swiftly from
the driver's seat and hurried towards her.

'No, I'm merely out of breath.' Not bothering with
explanations, she turned on her heel and ran to the
main door, hurrying inside. Her heart lurched painfully, guilt sweeping over her at the sight of her
niece's wan face, the large eyes so like her own a
picture of accusation. Emma was the only child
remaining in the playroom. Even her dark blue
dungarees and red top looked woebegone, and as
Jane hurried to her and swung the little girl into her
arms she was close to tears herself.

'You been long ages,' Emma said gruffly, holding
herself stiffly in Jane's clasp.

'I'm sorry, darling, my silly car wouldn't start.
Come on, we'll get some special cakes for tea on the
way home.'

Hugging Emma to her, Jane bade a quick farewell
to the nursery assistant and left the building.

'It's the last thing you need,' Jane murmured softly against Emma's cheek. 'But you knew I wouldn't forget you, didn't you?'

Gravely Emma nodded, as Jane stood her down on the ground. 'Come on, race you to the gate.' After a moment, Emma trotted beside her, but before they could move more than a few steps, a familiar deep voice came from the edge of the pavement. Matthew still waited beside his car.

'Can I give you and your little girl a lift? If the return journey exhausts you as much as the one here, *you'll* be a suitable candidate for coronary care by the time you get home.'

'No, thanks, we're fine.' Jane was acutely conscious of her dishevelled appearance. Blast, she thought, embarrassment making her flustered. I didn't even comb my hair or clean my teeth before I came out. And of course, he looks immaculate. She glanced sideways at Matthew's crisp white shirt and designer jeans, a broad leather belt emphasising the trim line of his waist and hips.

'It would be no trouble. As a matter of fact, I'm at a bit of a loose end for the next hour or so. I'd be glad of the company.'

'Oh, well, if that's the case, thank you very much.'

Bowing a little ironically, as Matthew held the door open, Jane lifted Emma into the rear seat of the car and climbed in beside her.

'Is it far to your house?' Matthew settled himself comfortably behind the steering-wheel and looked at Jane through the rear-view mirror.

'No distance at all. Just past the next corner on the left and down the hill.' Carefully, Jane clicked both her own and Emma's seatbelts into place before grinning back at Matthew. 'When you see how steep the hill is,' she added, 'you'll understand why I looked as though I was gasping my last, after climbing it in a hurry.'

He smiled in answer as he pulled away from the kerb, moving in the direction Jane had indicated.

'I didn't realise you had a little girl.'

'She's not. . .' Jane began, then she stopped, a wariness deep inside preventing further explanations. Raw after the death of her sister, she couldn't face the idea of any sort of emotional entanglement. Though who said anything about emotional entanglement? she told herself sharply. Perhaps she was over-reacting to Matthew's offers of help, but all she sought at the present time was some measure of peace for her mother, the children and herself. Instinctively she jibbed at the idea of letting him know too much about her personal life; and she certainly didn't want him to feel sorry for her. Which he could well do, if he knew her circumstances.

'Auntie Jane,' Emma piped up suddenly, her small voice clear above the soft purring of the car's engine. 'I did finger painting today, one for you and one for Grandma,' and she spread multicoloured hands for Jane's inspection.

Oh, my God, Jane thought, staring at the paint-splattered palms in horror. In this car, too. 'Whatever you do,' she hissed quietly, 'make sure you don't get any on the seat.' She seized Emma's hands and held them firmly in her own.

'Auntie Jane, eh?' Matthew's curiosity was plain

from his tone but still Jane offered no details. It would be too easy to become involved with someone like Matthew, she thought. He had such an air of quiet confidence and certainly a great deal of charm.

But despite her good intentions she couldn't prevent an appreciative glance at the broad back in front of her and felt an unexpected urge to touch the dark springy hair in the nape of his neck.

Whatever's the matter with me? she thought, her eyes wide. She had to stifle a giggle as she wondered what Matthew's reaction would be if she gave way to her impulse.

'How old is she?' His voice interrupted her tangled musings.

'I'm three years old and I'm called Emma. I live with Auntie Jane and Grandma. I got a brother. . .' To Jane's relief, Emma suddenly lost interest in the conversation, her attention drawn to a bicycle on the pavement. She pulled absent-mindedly at her hair, dislodging the red ribbon, and quickly Jane busied herself with retying the narrow strip of silk. But if Matthew noticed Jane's unwillingness to give any more details about their family he gave no sign. After a pause, while he threaded his way round a group of cars, he glanced again at them both through the rear-view mirror.

'And if you're interested, Emma, I'm Matthew John Guimaraes de Carvalho and I won't say how old I am, but it's just ten times your age,' he laughed.

'Good heavens, what an impressive name.' Jane grimaced. 'I'm just Jane. Oh, we're nearly there.' Quickly she leapt forward and tapped Matthew on the shoulder. 'At the end of that row of houses,' she cut in hastily. The big car slid quietly to a stop and, like a well trained chauffeur, Matthew moved quickly from the driver's seat and flung open the rear door.

'Thank you.' Hastily Jane climbed from the car, then lifted Emma, hugging the little girl close as a protection against the intensity of Matthew's dark-eyed stare.

'Would you like to come in for coffee or tea or something?' She couldn't for the life of her imagine what the 'something' would be. There might be sherry at the back of the cupboard but in any case, the problem of hospitality didn't arise as Matthew shook his head.

'Another time maybe; I have to get back to the hospital. See you at work tonight?'

'No, I have a few nights off now.' Jane didn't know if she was glad or sorry that Matthew wasn't able to stay. Perhaps it was better like this, she thought. As it was, she could sense a small twitch of the living-room curtains from behind her and she turned quickly towards the house, with Emma in her arms, as Matthew opened the wooden gate to let them through.

'If you need a lift again, if your car gives trouble, ring me. You know my bleep number, don't you?'

Matthew bent and flicked Emma gently on the cheek with his forefinger and smiled at them both, before opening his car door. Sighing to herself, she didn't know why, Jane went into the house.

'Saw you had a lift.' Her mother's face was the picture of curiosity as Jane knelt and removed

Emma's shoes, putting on blue bunny slippers, before fetching the little girl a drink of orange juice.

'That was the doctor I told you about,' Jane smiled. 'That's the car that caused all the trouble.'

'Well, it was very nice of him to give you a lift. You still look tired despite your sleep.'

'I feel it.' Jane yawned widely. 'I was glad not to have to walk back, I must admit it. It's a bit of a drag with a little one in tow.'

'I'll get us all something to eat while you have a shower and change.' Mrs Shelby got painfully to her feet and limped across the room to the kitchen door.

'A shower is a good idea, but leave the tea, Mum. I'll do it when I get down again. You put your feet up.'

'I only get stiff if I sit around, you know that. It may take me longer than you, but it's all good therapy. At least, that's what the specialist said.'

Jane shook her head in admiration, before picking up Emma's small brightly coloured bag and moving into the hall. She paused at the bottom stair, metallic noises and the sound of an occasional thud drawing her to the front door.

Oh, no, not someone tampering with her car. There wasn't usually any trouble with vandals in this area, but. . . Jane hurried outside.

'What on earth are you doing?' Surprise at seeing him made her voice sharper than she intended as she gazed through the front gate to where a tousle-haired Matthew was just visible above the hedge. He gave a cheerful grin as he held a spanner aloft.

'Just fixing your car. You had some dirt on the

plugs and then flooded it with too much choke, that's why it wouldn't start.'

He disappeared from view and the sound of her car engine rose in the air.

I flooded it, thought Jane, seething as she hurried to the front gate. Silly little me!

'There was no need for you to have done that. I'm quite capable of organising someone from the local garage.' He really was just so. . .she spluttered inwardly, just so. . .high-handed.

'I knew if I suggested it you'd say don't bother.' Matthew climbed smoothly from the front of the Mini. A streak of oil on one cheek added to his appearance of a mischievous small boy as he wiped his hands on a tissue, then stared down at her, one elbow resting on the roof of her car.

'You do like organising, don't you?'

'What's wrong with that?'

'Nothing. Sorry I snapped.' Jane shook her head in disbelief. Whatever was the matter with her? 'Anyway, thank you. Do you want to come in and wash your hands?' she added more graciously.

'No thanks. I must get a move on.'

'I am grateful for your help. . . Oh, do you know you've got some oil on your face?' She reached up and rubbed at the mark with her thumb, as unthinking as if it were Harry or Emma. But she jumped back, feeling as though she'd been scalded as she touched the slightly prickly surface of Matthew's cheek. It didn't help her quivering senses that the smell of his aftershave seemed to cling to her fingers.

'Have I?' He scrubbed busily at it with a tissue. 'That better?' He leant towards her and Jane had to clasp her hands firmly behind her back as she struggled to control a wish to smooth one finger down Matthew's face, so close to her own.

'Yes, that's fine,' she muttered breathlessly. 'I must go. Sorry if I was a bit abrupt.' Not waiting for him to answer, she hurried indoors to her overdue shower, wishing she'd had one before fetching Emma from nursery. She'd felt distinctly at a disadvantage being so ill-kempt as they'd driven home. And Matthew had managed to look well-groomed, even while working on her car, she thought with a rueful grin.

It was nice of him to help, she thought, stripping off her clothes and stepping under the stream of hot water, and she could have been a little more grateful. But there would be no need to take up his offer of a lift. Now that he'd fixed her car, she could be independent once more, for which she was truly thankful. Wasn't she? Surely that wasn't an edge of disappointment she felt at not having to call on him?

Briskly rubbing herself dry, spraying on some of her favourite cologne and dressed in a bright yellow tracksuit, Jane hurried back to the kitchen. She had started to spend a fixed time with the two children before they had their tea. Harry wasn't so much of a problem, for he seemed to be his usual self, noisy, demanding and full of beans.

But Emma, at three, was able to understand enough to make it far more difficult and still cried for her Mummy if upset.

I hope I'm doing right, Jane fretted, as she had done so often, about the best way to tackle Emma's loss. Perhaps it wasn't ideal to establish a routine that completely excluded Emma's parents, but so far, it was all Jane could think of to help Emma with her grief.

It didn't take long for them to finish their tea. Both children were obviously hungry and enjoyed their scrambled eggs on toast.

'Right, it's story-time.' Once they'd finished eating, Jane wiped the children's hands and faces. 'I think we'll have to scrub that with a scrubbing brush at bath-time,' she said, pointing to Emma's still heavily stained fingers, and was pleased at the little girl's giggle in answer. Harry in her arms, Jane returned to the sitting-room, sat back on the settee and without being told Emma climbed beside her, snuggling close to her aunt.

'What shall it be today, Emma?' The little girl shrugged, her eyes, wide with anticipation, so like her mother's that it brought a lump to Jane's throat.

She thought back to the Emma she'd known when Emma's parents were alive, exuberant and barely able to sit still for longer than five minutes. Now she was quiet and biddable, agreeing to everything that Jane asked. Too biddable at times, and Jane sighed to herself as she opened the book of fairy-tales and began reading Emma's favourite, *Cinderella*. Before long, Harry had fallen asleep, his small rosebud mouth trembling softly with each breath.

Putting a warning finger to her lips, Jane carefully carried the little boy upstairs and laid him in his cot, his yellow all-in-one sleepsuit fitting snugly to his well spread legs.

Tiptoeing from the room, Jane returned to the sitting-room. 'Now that there are just the two of us,

Emma, do you want to play a game or would you like to watch some television?'

Emma, her thumb tucked into the corner of her mouth, thought for a moment before wriggling down from the settee and switching on the set. To Jane's relief, they were lucky enough to catch part of a cartoon, and Emma was soon absorbed in the antics of the spotted dog and his friend as they flashed up on the screen.

Moving quietly to the kitchen, Jane sank down thankfully on to the wooden seat and watched as her mother dropped the final potatoes into the saucepan.

'God, I'm tired.' Pushing her hands through her short fair hair, Jane ignored the look of concern on her mother's face as she filled the kettle and put mugs on the table.

'Just relax for five minutes, while you have your coffee. Emma will soon call us if she needs us.'

'I must admit, suddenly being hurtled into motherhood is a bit of a shock, isn't it? Not that I've any reservations about doing it and I know you haven't.' Hastily, Jane reached out and patted her mother's arm.

'I wish I could do more. If only David had made a will, the financial situation would be easier, you wouldn't have to work and the load would be a lot lighter for us both.'

'You're more than pulling your weight, so there's no need to think otherwise. And to be quite truthful I'd hate to not work at all. It's a help for me, helps me to forget at least some of the time about Penny and David.' Jane finished her coffee then took her empty cup to the sink, rinsing it under the tap.

'Don't worry about the money. Mr Lorrimer the solicitor said we could have an advance if things get desperate. And you can't really blame David that he didn't make a will, can you? What thirty-year-old expects. . .?' Jane stopped in mid-flow. 'Anyway, enough of that. What else needs to be done?'

'It's all more or less ready. I'll just make sure Emma is all right, then we'll have our meal. You can relax in front of the television for the rest of the evening. That detective series you like is on tonight, isn't it?'

Jane laid the table as her mother left the kitchen. There was a murmur of voices and the sound of a theme tune as the door opened, then silence. Jane took the pie from the oven and strained the vegetables, amazed once again at how well her mother seemed to be coping. Mrs Shelby's health might be poor, the arthritis in her hands giving her enough pain to make her cringe at times, but in other ways she'd been a tower of strength since her elder daughter's untimely death.

Jane dished up the meat pie and potatoes, ladled peas on to each plate and was surprised at how hungry she felt once they'd started eating. There was a comfortable silence during the course of the meal. But once the plates were empty Mrs Shelby pushed hers aside and rested her elbows on the table, an inquisitive light in her eyes.

'Right, I'm all ears. Tell me what happened at work. We've hardly had time to talk to one another over the last couple of days.'

'What do you want to hear?' Jane thought back over her nights on duty. It had been easier in some ways than she'd expected, much harder in others. The most vivid impressions had come from working with Matthew. Despite some awkward moments, her original doubts had soon faded and she found herself looking forward to the time she spent in his company. But there was no need to mention this to her mother.

She knew how anxious the older woman was that Jane wouldn't get the chance to enjoy a social life, indeed she'd mentioned it earlier, and if Jane suggested any sort of liking for the registrar her mother would go to all sorts of lengths to try to arrange free time for Jane.

And she didn't want that.

'Well,' Jane began, pushing her back more comfortably against one of the padded cushions, 'there are six beds in CCU.'

'CCU?' her mother queried.

'Coronary Care. But we only had four patients on the first two nights. Two were discharged, both heart attacks doing well, but we kept the other two: one lady, one man. He's the most poorly, suffers from angina, which seems to be getting worse. Only forty years old, as well. They were saying he might have surgery, but I hope not. He's got a young family.'

Jane pushed her hand through her hair. 'He was very interested to hear about Emma and Harry.'

She was silent, thinking back to how reassuring Matthew had been with Mr Jennings, very gentle as he explained to the man's wife what was happening, his deep blue eyes full of concern. And his kindness towards herself, giving her a lift, repairing her car, wasn't necessarily interference, just the sign of someone with a good heart. Quickly, she shrugged off such thoughts. It was a dangerous road they were travelling along, to keep dwelling on his good points.

'I think it'll take a bit of getting used to,' Jane said as her mother waited patiently for her to continue, 'but I'm sure I'll enjoy it. It's nice having few enough patients to get to know them, rather than glossing over the surface.'

'But what about the primary care you were telling me about? When each nurse is responsible for a certain number of patients right the way through their stay in hospital?'

'Well, in a way, it's all primary care in the unit, because there are so few patients in number. And in fact a lot of them only stay for a few days, before being transferred.'

'Well, I'm glad you're settling in. . . Oh, hello, Emma, what's the matter?'

'I'm lonely.'

Jane swung on her chair and held out her arms as the kitchen door opened. 'Come on, little one, up with me. Grandma and I were just having a chat. Do you want to have a cup of tea with us?'

'Yes, please.' Emma scrambled up beside her aunt as Mrs Shelby filled the kettle and plugged it in.

'Don't you want to watch any more television?'

Emma shook her head. 'I want to go to bed.'

'Well, as soon as you've had your drink, it'll be bathtime anyway, and we've got to get a big scrubbing brush, to get this off your hands, haven't we?' She tickled her niece's palm, bringing a smile to the little girl's lips.

* * *

'Leave the washing-up, Mum.' Gently pushing her mother from the kitchen, Jane ran hot water into the bowl and quickly rinsed out their few plates, then followed her mother to the sitting-room.

Light-headed despite her day's sleep, at first Jane found it difficult to concentrate on the television play.

'I'm glad Matthew was able to fix my car for me.' Her voice low, Jane was more or less speaking to herself. 'I must admit, I wouldn't like to try and get to work by public transport. Two buses to the hospital and the second one only runs every half-hour.' She paused thoughtfully. 'I must thank him properly, the next time I see him.'

Her mother pulled a face, her mouth a humorous twist as she studied her daughter.

'Are you sure there isn't more to this Matthew than you've told me?'

'Nothing to get in a tizzy about, Mum, I promise you. I don't even particularly like the man. But I must admit I was very grateful to see him this afternoon.' Jane giggled at the memory. 'Tell you what, you couldn't imagine anything less romantic than the sight of me hanging on to the gatepost at the nursery, all red-faced, trying to get my breath back. I ran most of the way up Nover's hill, afraid I'd be late for Emma, and you know how steep that is.'

With an absorbed expression Jane turned and gazed intently at the screen. She didn't want to talk about Matthew, afraid perhaps of revealing to her mother's astute gaze something that she'd not even admitted to herself. Once again, she recalled the warmth she felt when Matthew was around, which she had difficulty in disguising. Her only recourse seemed to be to snap at him, which she didn't want to do. He must think she was a terrible misery. She pictured again the way his eyes seemed to bore into her and his gentle touch with Emma.

Ignoring her mother's expression of surprise, Jane turned up the volume on the set. Perhaps the blast of sound would drag her attention back to the screen and stop it wandering to a broad-shouldered man who seemed to have the knack of cropping up in her thoughts whenever she least expected it. But her hopes were not realised, for Matthew not only continued to fill her mind that evening, but also haunted her dreams, when she gave up all pretence of watching television and finally went to bed.

CHAPTER FOUR

'WELL, I hope the night keeps quiet for you.' Anne Golding, the staff nurse on day duty, smiled a farewell, looking back from the door of the ward as she closed it gently behind her. Jane sighed. It seemed too much to hope for lately — a quiet night. Despite a day's sleep, she felt more tired than she had when she'd gone to bed that morning.

In fact if it stayed as quiet as this, she thought, it would suit her very well. She glanced at the peaceful unit with the monitors occasionally flashing colour like small floral blooms and the flowered curtains shielding the patients, some of whom were already sleeping, two with their heads at exactly the same angle on their banked-up pillows.

'Come on, let's get everything done as soon as we can, then settle ourselves as well,' Sally laughed. 'I reckon I wouldn't take a lot of rocking myself tonight.'

'Nor me.' Jane yawned hugely, following her friend to the central desk area. 'It's nice to have you back on nights.' She collected the medicine list and patients charts.

'I'll get the drinks, you do night-time drugs,' Sally said briskly, moving towards the kitchen, her thick dark hair, in its clip at the nape of her neck, bouncing with the energy of her walk.

God, she makes me feel weary, just looking at

54

her. Jane grinned to herself as she set out injection trays and medicine pots and collected the various drugs, ready to check them with Sally when the other nurse returned. It didn't take long to hand round the few tablets and give the only two injections that were prescribed.

'Mrs Gregson has the knack of wanting whatever I haven't got with me in the drinks line,' grumbled Sally softly. 'Means I always have to go back to the kitchen. Oh, well, now that they've had their drinks, we can have ours. How have you been?'

'The past couple of weeks has been pretty hectic. How come you're on nights again, by the way?'

'No one else to do it. Go on—you were saying?'

'Well, you know how busy we've been in here?'

Sally nodded sympathetically.

'I've thoroughly enjoyed it, don't get me wrong, but with all I've got going on at home it seems a never-ending round of—I don't know—not drudgery exactly, but, well. . .oh, I shouldn't complain.'

'Of course you must, if it makes you feel better.' Sally refilled their coffee-cups from the pot on the desk and without asking put a heaped spoonful of sugar into Jane's.

Thoughtfully, Jane sipped at her drink. She'd not been very happy leaving her mother this evening, for her mother had suffered more than usual in the recent wet weather that had chased away all signs of spring and brought with it howling winds and heavy downpours, making the grey skies look more like November than April.

Still, it was no use worrying. As long as they both managed to keep going, once David's small estate had been sorted out, they could go somewhere warm for a complete break. But at the moment finances were too tight to think of anything other than the basics and Jane frowned again, the sudden lowering of her spirits a reflection of the dull evening that had darkened unusually early in the storms.

'Hello, how's my favourite nurse?' A familiar voice greeted Jane as she hurried to the first cubicle, in answer to the bell.

'Mr Jennings, I'm sorry to see you back again,' Jane tutted. 'You promised me you would take care of yourself, after that last attack. I hope this doesn't mean that you've slipped into bad habits.'

'Course not,' His grey-tinged face attempted a smile that was only partly successful. 'I said I wanted to see you again and they said that the only way I'd get past the hordes of admirers would be to come in as a patient once more.'

'Hordes of admirers!' Jane spluttered. 'Chance would be a fine thing. You're my only admirer at present. Not that I'm complaining.' Gently, she squeezed his hand. 'Quality rather than quantity, any day.'

She studied her patient carefully as she shook tablets into the medicine pot and placed it on the bedside locker. 'Just some temazepan for you tonight, make sure you get a good night's sleep. Have you got any chest pain at the moment?'

He shook his head. 'Nothing that a galloping horse would notice, thanks, love.'

Jane glanced at him shrewdly. 'If I'm not mistaken, that means that you have still got pain. I'm going to get the doctor to take a look at you before we settle you down for the night.'

Carefully, Jane counted his pulse, feeling a twinge of distress at the thin, thready beat, but the monitor showed no obvious problems. 'Nothing to worry about at the moment, but I'll still be happier if we get everything checked to make sure. So no arguing.' She smiled to take the sting from her words and walked swiftly to the board to see which of the medical staff was covering the unit.

'Hmm,' she muttered. 'Our friend Dr Carvalho. Well, he always calls in last thing anyway.'

She hadn't seen anything of Matthew during her last two weeks of duty. The hospital grapevine reported that he'd gone away on a course and in the darkest reaches of the night she thought sometimes that his absence hadn't done anything to help her depression.

She hated to admit it, but she'd missed Matthew far more than she would have thought possible, and she hurried to the duty roster every time she worked, to see if he was the one on call.

'I'm just going to get Matthew to come and see Mr Jennings,' Jane mouthed to Sally over the edge of the telephone in answer to Sally's enquiring stare.

She dialled in Matthew's bleep numbers, unable to control a moment's breathlessness as she waited for him to ring back.

But an impatient buzzer dragged her from the phone to a bedside.

'Sally, can you come here a minute?' Jane barely managed to keep the panic from her voice at the sight of Mrs Meadows hunched forward in her bed, her breath rasping in her throat, her face the picture of anxiety.

'Nurse, I can't breathe.'

Jane hurriedly picked up the stethoscope, glancing at the monitor screen as she did so.

'Any pain, Mrs Meadows?' She could hear a wheeze as she listened, as she imagined the noise of old-fashioned bellows would be.

'No pain, but I feel as though my lungs have closed over,' the frightened woman muttered.

'I'm waiting for the doctor to get here. He'll see you as soon as he arrives.'

'Did you want me, Jane? What's the problem?'

She swung on her heel as Matthew's voice broke into her worried thoughts.

'Sounds like left ventricular failure. I think she's got some pulmonary oedema,' Jane muttered softly. 'Her lungs sound really wet.'

'Could be right.' Matthew smiled reassuringly at Mrs Meadows, carefully warming the end of the stethoscope in the palm of his hand, before listening to her chest.

'Do you want a diuretic to get rid of all that fluid? What—frusemide?' Jane raised her eyebrows enquiringly as Matthew finished his examination.

'Yes, please, and we'll have an ECG and a chest X-ray.' He moved swiftly from the bed to the telephone on the desk. 'Was that why you bleeped me?' He turned to face her and Jane paused, over-whelmed at how pleased she was to see him. For a moment she couldn't answer, feasting her eyes on the strong dark face, the broad shoulders shown to advantage in a dark grey suit, his olive skin emphasised by the whiteness of his shirt.

'Jane, did you hear what I said?' He snapped his fingers.

'Sorry. Mr Jennings has some chest pain and though he says it isn't severe, he's so uncomplaining I'm not very happy to take what he says as true.'

'"Welcome back,"' Matthew said with a wry grin. 'I don't know, I'm away for a couple of weeks and what happens?' He shook his head in disbelief as he went to the first side-ward, Jane following close behind.

'Well, Mr Jennings, I believe the pain is giving you problems.' Carefully, Matthew took hold of his patient's wrist, studying the wave-form on the monitor at the same time. 'Mm, looks as though I'd better have a more thorough look at you. Jane, would you mind helping Mr Jennings take off his pyjama jacket, while I go and ring X-Ray?'

He spun on his heel and left them, the set of his shoulders looking, Jane had to admit to herself, weary when compared with the vibrant energy that usually seemed to surround him.

It was a bit grim, she thought, sympathetically, one day back and nothing but problems waiting.

'Here you are, Mr Jennings, cover yourself with this blanket while I get the ECG machine.'

'Is that your boyfriend?' He gave a lop-sided grin, struggling manfully with a pain he could no longer hide.

'Don't be daft, he has better things to do than to bother with the. . . Are you all right?' Jane said abruptly. For Cliff Jennings' face changed colour as she watched and the wave-form on the monitor shot off into a staggered pattern, a long way from normal.

'Can you come here?' Jane rushed into the curtained area on the other side of the ward and seized Matthew's arm. 'Cliff is much worse.' Jane wondered why Matthew looked at her so strangely, then realised she had his arm in such a strong grip, she'd crumpled the edge of his sleeve.

'Sorry,' she muttered, red-faced, letting go as though the material were scorching hot.

'Not to worry.' He walked unhurriedly to Mr Jennings' bed and took one look at the man who was now sweating and grey.

'Have the defibrillator ready in case, and get me some morphine. I think he might have had another coronary.'

Anxiously Jane pushed the defibrillator trolley to the curtain, just out of sight of the patient.

'Sally, can you see to Mrs Meadows?' Jane muttered as her friend appeared with another tray of coffee.

'Sorry I've been so long. . .' She stared at the activity in the unit. 'What's been going on while I've been away? I only went to try and scrounge some milk and got chatting.' She moved swiftly to the other bed and Jane could hear Sally's soothing tones murmuring in comfort.

'Hang on with the defib. His heart rate is steadying.' Matthew looked at the monitor. 'We'll start an amiodarone infusion, that may be enough to settle the rhythm.'

Quickly Jane assembled the infusion, watching it run into one of the veins at the front of Cliff's arms.

'There you are, all going along nicely.'

Matthew gave the worried man a reassuring pat as he hurried to the other cubicle.

'All go here tonight,' he muttered. 'Still, it was sharp of you to spot the way Mr Jennings had deteriorated.'

Jane felt a glow of pleasure at the compliment, casually though Matthew had spoken. By the time she'd finished, Sally and Matthew had dealt with Mrs Meadows and the elderly woman lay back against her pillow, breathing more easily through the oxygen mask.

'I think we could do with a coffee after all that,' Sally sighed.

'I'll get some fresh.' Jane jumped to her feet and hurried to the tiny kitchen, plugging in the percolator and shaking ground coffee into the metal top.

By the time it had perked and was throwing out an appetising smell, she had found a few biscuits in the tin, setting them out on a plate.

'Don't know how these escaped the eagle eyes of the late shift,' Jane laughed, pointing to the small display on the tray. 'Black for you, Matthew?'

He nodded and stretched out in his chair, his arms folded behind his head, his eyes half closed. He'd loosened his tie and seemed relaxed, though there were shadows above the strong cheekbones, making him appear vulnerable; it was the first time Jane had seen him look tired. He always seemed to be completely in command, everything under his control, and his weariness now made him much more human in her eyes, and, she had to admit, very endearing.

'Lucky you were around just then.' Sally nodded

towards their doctor. 'It's unusual to have two emergencies at the same time, and, of course, I was missing.' She grimaced apologetically.

'Don't fret, Jane was coping very well.' He smiled his thanks as he took the coffee. 'Mm, I need that; I didn't have time for any dinner this evening. It's certainly not my day. I got home to find my house awash, all the downstairs carpets soaking from a burst water pipe; I couldn't stop to sort it out.'

'Oh, no, what are you going to do?' Jane's heart went out to him; no wonder he looked so tired.

'I haven't had time to do anything as yet. I plan to stay in the doctors' mess for the time being.'

It was just as well that Jane didn't stop to think before she spoke, for she'd never have had the courage. But the words just seemed to force their way from her mouth and even as she finished speaking she could feel embarrassment curling her whole body.

'Why don't you come and stay with us? We've got a spare room and even our little house must be more comfortable than the doctors' residence. You won't get any sleep there, being on the main road.'

Matthew let his chair fall forward on to the two front legs and stared at her in surprise. 'I couldn't possibly impose on you and your mother, but it's very kind of you to offer,' he finished, with a formal little bow from the waist.

'Fair enough.' Jane shrugged, not sure if she were glad or sorry that he'd refused. Perhaps it was just as well, she thought, getting to her feet and walking softly to the bedsides of their two sick patients. She might find it more of a strain than she could cope with, having Matthew under the same roof. It was bad enough when they were on duty, trying to hide how attracted she felt. In the enforced intimacies of living together. . . She shrugged the thought away. Both patients were sleeping peacefully, Mrs Meadows' breaths making a small rattle against the confines of the oxygen mask.

'Do you want more coffee?' Sally picked up the tray, stacking the mugs and jug tidily, as Jane returned to the desk area. 'I might as well finish that,' she added, picking up the last shortbread.

'No more coffee for me, thanks.' Jane shook her head. She was silent as Sally took the tray back to the kitchen, shy now that she and Matthew were alone, apart from four sleeping patients, of course.

'That was very kind of you, to ask me to stay.' Matthew rested his elbows on the desk and stared at her. 'I must say, I was quite taken aback — I had the impression that you didn't like me all that much.'

'Whatever gave you that idea?' Jane squeaked.

'Well, if you don't mind my saying so,' he smiled apologetically, 'you do answer rather sharply at times, and very often, you look as though you wish I were a million miles away. What is called a baleful look from those green eyes, like a malevolent cat.'

'I do no such thing,' Jane spluttered. 'I've never been malevolent in my life. I'm not even sure what it means.'

'Perhaps I've been unduly sensitive.' He knuckled his eyes, giving a huge yawn. 'God, I'm tired.'

'London is exhausting, isn't it? Especially driving in all that traffic.'

'I didn't take my car. It's not worth the bother in London.'

'And you never know if some vandal might attack it,' Jane grinned mischievously, moving her chair to make room for Sally to sit down.

'Now, you don't still hold that against me, surely,' Matthew remonstrated, struggling with a smile that wouldn't go away.

'Here, what's going on here with you two? Let me in on the joke.' Sally's tone was plaintive.

'It's just that the first time Matthew saw me, he thought I was mistreating his precious car.'

'Oh, I remember, you mentioned it.' Sally still looked puzzled. 'I can't quite see what's funny.'

'Nor can I.' Jane picked up a file and began to turn over the pages of notes.

'It was only funny in retrospect,' Matthew explained. 'You should have seen Jane, like an angry bantam, her feathers well and truly ruffled. . .'

'I don't know about angry; I was terrified. The way you loomed over me. . .'

She broke off, suddenly aware of the way Matthew was looking at her.

'Jane, I would never want to frighten you. You weren't really scared, were you?' He reached across the desk and took her hand in his, gently rubbing his thumb across the sensitive skin of her wrist. She snatched her hand free, partly because of the interest Sally was showing, partly because she thought she'd never known anything more sensual than Matthew's touch.

He raised his eyebrows as Jane pulled away but didn't comment.

'By the way, I thought of it today when I was

travelling to London. Have your little ones ever been on a train?'

'No.'

'Well, there's an excursion at the end of next week. How would you fancy a day-trip? It's only about an hour's ride each way so wouldn't be too much for them.'

'I'm sure they'd love it. Thank you.'

'That's great. I'll organise it and let you know the details.' He got to his feet. 'Now, despite the coffee and biscuit, I'm starving, so I'm off to get something to eat. I'll be back before I go to bed but both patients seem stable now and hopefully won't cause any more problems.'

'Touch wood when you say that,' Jane instructed, slapping her hand noisily on the surface of the desk.

'Call me if you're worried. I'll have my bleep. Thanks again for the coffee.'

He strode from the ward, turning to lift a hand in farewell as he reached the ward door and disappeared from view.

'Right, give.' Sally perched on the edge of the desk, pushing aside the heap of charts.

'What do you mean?' Jane stared back, wide-eyed.

'Don't play the innocent with me. I didn't know you and Matthew were, quote, good friends, unquote.'

'For heavens sake, "friends" sums it up. Don't say anything to suggest otherwise, particularly not when Matthew's around.' Jane's voice rose in protest. 'The only time I've seen him, away from work, was when he gave me a lift. I'd die, if I thought he heard even a hint. . .'

'All right, all right, don't get in such a state. I only asked as you appeared to get on so well.' Sally leaned back in her chair and looked at Jane knowingly. 'I think he feels more than you're letting on and I also think that you are protesting too much.'

'Honestly, Sally, the only time I've seen him, apart from work, was when he gave Emma and me a lift. He was interested to know that Mum and I have the care of the two childrem, but even then I didn't tell him about Penny and David.'

'Why the invitation, then?'

Jane shrugged. 'I should think it's just that he loves kids and fancied the opportunity to spend some time with my little horrors.'

'Wonder why he's never married?' Sally frowned.

'I don't know. I must admit it's puzzled me at times.' As well as being very attractive, Matthew had looked so relaxed and at ease with Emma, it seemed a shame that he hadn't got a family of his own.

'Oh, well, nothing to do with us.' Sally shrugged. 'He must appreciate the way you care for Emma and Harry, though, or he wouldn't bother to ask you out. I think you're a saint,' she continued, opening one of the files and taking out address labels. 'I'm sure I couldn't take on the responsibility for a couple of children and still keep working.'

'Needs must, I'm afraid. And it's with my mother's help and guidance. Besides, I love Emma and Harry to bits.' Jane paused, surprised at how true the statement was.

Of course, being tied made her resentful at times, and on one occasion she'd been horrified at the wave of anger that had swept over her. Not anger at the children but a fierce heat of rage at Penny and David for leaving her to cope. Although anger was a natural part of grief, knowing it hadn't stopped the guilt Jane had suffered afterwards.

'Anyway, enough of my problems.' Swiftly, Jane flipped open the pages on the days report. 'I wonder why Cliff Jennings should suddenly develop complications like that?'

'Probably had another infarct. It happens sometimes; I can't see him getting away without some sort of surgery. Bit ironic; you think someone is getting over their heart attack and just as you relax, bang! there goes another.'

'That's not very encouraging,' Jane grimaced.

'It doesn't happen that often; I didn't express myself very well.' Sally sighed. 'But it makes you wonder if we're doing the right thing here with these coronary patients. After all, they should be having absolute peace and freedom from stress and very often all they see are other people with the same condition, perhaps having worse problems than their own. It must be very distressing for them.'

'But that must be outweighed by the confidence of knowing that they're in the place with all the expert care available, surely?'

'Possibly,' Sally murmured doubtfully. 'It would be interesting to have a study done, to find out just how much it benefits someone to be in a unit like this.'

'I'm sure that if I had anything wrong with my

heart, God forbid, I'd like to know I'd got people like you and me and Matthew around to sort me out.'

'Well said, Jane.' Both nurses swung round at the sound of Matthew's voice. 'And I promise you faithfully, if ever such an eventuality did come about, you would have my undivided attention as long as it was necessary.'

'That's good to know.' Hastily, Jane turned again to the patients notes and stared at them, though she barely took in the meaning of the words on the page. The thought of undivided attention of any sort from Matthew Carvalho was enough to cause her heart to flutter nervously like some trapped bird.

What was she thinking of, getting in such a tizzy? He wasn't suggesting anything more than that he would take care of her if she was a patient. But she couldn't control a rush of feeling that frightened her with its intensity as he stood beside her. She could sense the warmth of his arm close to her own and smell his expensive cologne, which made her nostrils dilate, even as she bent her head forward, pretending to be absorbed in her notes.

'Did you manage to get some supper?' Lazily, Sally stretched out one long leg and hooked a spare chair towards the desk. 'Here you are, take the weight off your feet.'

Jane stared, trying to control feelings of envy. Not only at the matter-of-fact way that Sally behaved in Matthew's presence but also at the sight of those long legs and the tall, slim height of her friend. No wonder no one notices me, Jane thought in sudden resentment. I'm such a shorty, anyone of normal height is bound to overlook me.

'Whatever are you muttering about to yourself?' Matthew leant on the desk and grinned into her face.

'Oh, was I muttering? Just thinking about something that annoyed me,' Jane said hastily.

'Hope it wasn't me. You looked fit enough to strangle whoever it was.'

Jane giggled, despite herself.

'It wasn't important.'

'That's a relief. Now to business. How are this evening's two problems?'

'Mr Jennings is certainly more comfortable.'

'No more pain in his chest?'

'Not since he had the morphine.'

'And what about Mrs Meadows? Is she passing plenty of urine now?'

'Loads,' Sally nodded. 'The frusemide has certainly worked.'

'Great. Looks as though we might be winning.'

'I told you earlier, touch wood,' Jane said quickly.

'Don't believe in all that mumbo-jumbo,' Matthew laughed. 'Give me the certainties of science any day.'

'I don't believe there are tree spirits that we have to placate every time we touch wood for luck,' Jane protested. 'But as Shakespeare said, "there are more things in heaven and earth, Horatio".'

'I suppose so.'

'Anyone want more coffee?' Sally stretched her arms above her head. 'Only instant this time though,

I'm afraid. I can't be bothered to fiddle with the percolator.'

'I won't, thank you.' Wearily, Matthew stood up. I'll just check on our two, then I'm away to my bed. It's been a long, tiring day and if I can snatch a few hours' sleep I'll be more than grateful. Come on, Jane, give me a report on what's going on while Sally does her stuff with the coffee-pot.' He held out a hand and pulled Jane to her feet. She had a sudden desire to know what he actually wore in bed, if anything, a vivid picture in her mind of his broad, slightly tanned shoulders above a snowy white duvet.

Bet he sleeps in the nude, she thought, staring after him as he led the way to the first cubicle.

Hastily she pushed the vision from her.

It would be just my luck for him to read my mind, and I wouldn't want to shock his sensibilities too much. She had to stifle a giggle as she pictured a series of cartoon-like figures, complete with balloons of speech. I'd better calm down, she told herself firmly. My thoughts are beginning to misbehave.

CHAPTER FIVE

'ARE you sure you don't mind, Mum?' Blinking as the afternoon sunlight poured through the open back door, Jane rested her elbows on the kitchen table and looked across at her mother. 'I don't know what mad impulse made me ask him to stay, and I must admit I don't think I really expected him to accept.'

'If you can't ask a friend here when you want, I should feel most offended.'

'Well, he's not exactly a friend. But it seemed the right thing to do at the time.' Jane pulled at her bottom lip. Maybe her mother had no doubts about the invitation, but her own feelings were much more confused.

When Matthew had stopped her in the corridor that morning, as he hurried off-duty, and said that if the invitation still stood he'd be delighted to accept, she'd been dismayed at how her treacherous heart had behaved, racing in sudden excitement.

'Of course,' she'd burbled. 'We'll see you later.' And her thoughts during the drive home had been a muddle of apprehension and keen anticipation.

'You'd better let him have your room, as it's got its own shower, and you can move in with me,' her mother muttered purposefully. 'I'll change the bedding while you get ready for work. What time is he arriving?'

'Don't honestly know. Whenever he finishes. I'm

not sure if he's on call tonight, but I'll ring him before I leave and we can sort out about a front door key.'

'Must say, I'm looking forward to it,' Muriel Shelby grinned. 'Haven't had a man about the house for so long; it'll make a lovely change.'

'Hope the children don't get on his nerves, but they can't be noisier than the doctors' mess.' Jane laughed. 'Matthew said it was worse than New York, what with ambulance sirens, vegetable lorries going to the market, added to which, the walls there are so thin, he was disturbed every time the phone rang in any of the rooms.'

'Can't be much fun for those that have to stay.'

Jane scraped her chair back from the table and put her cup in the sink. 'No, that's true.' She paused, staring into their small back garden and breathed at the scent of newly mown grass that drifted in through the open door. 'Mmm,' she muttered, 'makes you feel that summer is really on the way, when you hear the mowers start and can smell the cut grass, doesn't it? I'll see to my room. I've got plenty of time before I have to get ready for work.' Tugging at the waistband of her jeans, she ran up the stairs and went into her bedroom. Hope it's not too feminine, she thought, staring critically from the doorway. The white-painted ceiling sloped towards a casement window, where flower-sprigged curtains fluttered a welcome. The furniture, a mixture of old and new, shone with polish, but she had to admit to herself, though comfortable, it wouldn't win any prizes in an Ideal Home display.

'Never mind,' she told her reflection in the small

round mirror that perched unsteadily on a chest of drawers, 'it's got to be better than one of those institutional places in the doctors' mess.'

Seizing bundles of clothes from a blue-painted basket chair, she hurried to the bathroom and thrust them into the clothes-bin. Not everything needed to be washed, but it was the quickest way she could think of to tidy up. After all, she didn't know how long it would be before Matthew arrived.

Hastily, she scooped her few items of make-up and brush and comb on to a tray, carrying them into her mother's room and setting them on the old-fashioned dressing-table.

She enjoyed the flurry of activity as she fought with the duvet cover—at least that was a sober dark blue—then sprayed the surfaces of the furniture with lavender-scented polish and put fresh towels in her tiny shower cubicle. It had originally been a walk-in cupboard and was barely big enough to swing the proverbial cat, but it had a sunny appearance with its yellow-painted walls and also, of course, had the advantage of being private.

'All done, Mum.' Jane flew into the kitchen, her tiredness gone. The anticipation of Matthew's visit had sent her blood fizzing in her veins and she felt more alive at the moment than she'd felt for long ages, as Emma would put it.

'Wonder what they'll think?' Wiping the last of the cups and saucers, Jane flicked out the tea-towel and hung it over the rail.

'Wonder what who will think?' her mother murmured in an abstracted tone, peering intently into her favourite recipe book.

'Emma and Harry, about Matthew, of course.'

'I should think they'll find him as fascinating as you seem to,' her mother muttered drily, peering over the top of her glasses with a wicked glint in her eyes.

'Mum,' Jane said warningly. 'Don't you dare. . .'

'Don't I dare what?' But before Jane could say any more, they were interrupted by the sound of the doorbell, and as Jane hurried to the front door she could feel the rapid pitter-patter of her heart rise into her throat. It couldn't be Matthew already, not while she was dressed in her old jeans and a tatty T-shirt that had stretched so badly, it hardly fitted at all.

'Hope I'm not too early?' She couldn't see the expression on Matthew's face as the sun slanted shadows across the doorway, but the sound of his voice was enough to set Jane's heart racing once more.

'No—er, no, it's fine. Come in.' She stood with her back against the open door to let him pass and the smooth material of his jacket brushed her bare skin, setting a run of gooseflesh along her arm.

'Put your bag here in the hall, and I'll take you out to see Mum.' Nervously, Jane edged past. For goodness' sake, calm down, she told herself as she went through to the kitchen, Matthew following close behind her.

'Mmm, something smells good. It's very kind of you to take pity on me.' He leaned across the table and shook Muriel Shelby's outstretched hand. 'I hope I won't have to impose on you for too long.'

'You're very welcome.' Jane's mother seemed

suddenly shy, turning away to pick up the kettle and fill it from the tap. 'How about a cup of tea? Or coffee if you prefer?'

'I can't stay, I'm afraid. I just called round to deliver my bags, then I must get back to the hospital. I didn't want to risk getting tied up there and have to disturb you at some ungodly hour.'

'You're on call again, are you?' Jane grimaced in sympathy.

''Fraid so. Unfortunately, it goes with the territory.'

Jane glanced from under her lashes, acutely aware of how he seemed to fill the kitchen. He was so much at ease, one hand resting lightly on the edge of the table, that anyone coming in would think that she and her mother were the visitors, not him. 'I won't get in your way this evening, as I'll probably be working till late.'

Jane stifled a tremor of disappointment and moved away from the back door.

'Shall I show you your room?'

'If that's all right?'

'Auntie Jane, Auntie Jane.' The sound of Emma's cry burst in from the garden, stirring Jane into a flurry of anxiety.

'What is it?'

She raced outside, her mouth dry with apprehension.

'Emma, you little menace!'

Her niece was spread out on their tiny lawn, grimly holding on to the end of a very long worm. Jane yelped in horror, praying it would manage to escape from Emma's clutches.

'Emma, leave it. Oh, goodness, look at the state of you.'

Large grey-green eyes stared back at her from a totally mud-plastered face.

'Come here and say hello to our guest. It's Dr Carvalho, do you remember him?'

'Hello, Uncle Doctor.' To Jane's surprise, without a trace of her usual shyness, Emma scrambled to her feet and ran towards Matthew, wrapping her mud-streaked arms around his legs.

'No, Emma. . .' But it was too late. Large streaks of dirt smeared the light grey material of Matthew's trousers and, as Emma went to pull away, an extra trail covered each immaculate knee.

'Oh, I'm so sorry.' Almost purple with embarrassment, Jane brushed ineffectually at the mud. But she soon stopped when she realised how intimate her unthinking attempts at cleaning the marks might appear.

'Come into the kitchen; we've a clothes-brush there and should be able to get rid of the mud.' She turned towards the door. 'And as for you, young lady, the sooner you get upstairs and wash those grubby hands, the better.'

'Please, don't tell her off. She didn't mean any harm,' Matthew murmured softly as he stood close to Jane, the zephyr touch of his breath on her neck making her shiver.

'I'm sure Mum will be able to get it clean for you,' she gabbled.

Seizing Emma's wrist, Jane hurried indoors and couldn't prevent a giggle at the look on her mother's face, when she saw the dirt-smeared trousers of their guest, her horrified stare reflecting Jane's feelings exactly.

'Do you want to take your things upstairs?' Jane gestured towards the hall.

'I think I had better change, and then I really must be on my way.' He glanced at his watch. 'I've got Mr Jennings' angiograms to see from this morning; I'm afraid he seems worse.' Matthew sighed deeply. 'It's been one long rush today. Let's hope it quietens down before you get to work.'

'Uncle Doctor, are you going to live here?' For a moment, Jane had forgotten her niece and she turned with a start towards the small voice.

'Why do you call him Uncle Doctor?' She crouched down and put her face level with Emma's.

'We. . .ll.' The little girl started to put an abstracted finger into her mouth, frowning as Jane hurriedly pulled it away. 'I haven't got a uncle, and he's a doctor. . .' She gestured thoughtfully in Matthew's direction.

'I think it's a lovely idea.' As he leant forward, Matthew's face was only inches from Jane and Emma, and Jane breathed deeply at the fresh clean smell of his aftershave, its sharp tang sending a *frisson* of pleasure through her.

'And yes, Emma, in answer to your question, your aunt and grandma have very kindly asked me to stay here for a little while. You don't mind, do you?'

Emma shook her head, her eyes fixed firmly on Matthew's face so close to her own. Suddenly she leant forward and planted a noisy kiss on his cheek, then, overcome at her daring, turned and scrambled up the stairs as fast as her legs would carry her, the sound of her laughter spiralling down to the three adults in the kitchen.

'Well, you've certainly made a hit.' Eyebrows raised, Muriel Shelby gazed admiringly at Matthew.

'It's very kind of you to say so.' He grinned at the older woman. 'The trouble is that I only have that effect on the very young or the very old. I'm trying desperately to improve my technique, so that I can make a similar impact on people of my own age.' And Jane had to look away as Matthew's dark blue gaze stared intently in her direction. He couldn't be hinting. . .?

'Come on,' she said gruffly, pushing the thought aside. 'You'd better get yourself sorted if you've got to be back at the hospital.' As she hurried upstairs, acutely aware of the sound of his footsteps behind her, she couldn't help wondering if perhaps her impulsive invitation had been such a good idea.

But she gave no hint of her doubts as she opened the bedroom door and stood back to let Matthew pass.

'This all looks very comfortable.' He stepped into the room, putting his bag on the floor, and moved to the window. 'The air has almost a country smell, hasn't it?'

'I was saying to Mum earlier, that it's nice to have the scent of the freshly mown grass. Makes you feel summer is on the way.'

Matthew turned and surveyed the room, the large framed photograph on the bedside table catching his eye. He nodded towards it.

'What an attractive couple. Who are they?'

It was a snapshot of Penny and David during a

holiday they'd taken the previous year and they looked like teenagers, windblown and laughing at the camera.

Hastily, Jane picked it up and clutched it to her.

'Sorry, I'm so used to the photograph sitting there, I tend to overlook it.'

'There's no need to move it on my account,' Matthew said softly.

'It's my Mummy and Daddy. They've gone away and can't come back.'

Jane shivered at Emma's matter-of-fact tones as the little girl came in from the bathroom, bringing with her a smell of baby soap, though she looked no cleaner than before her wash.

There was silence for one long moment, Jane completely at a loss for words as Matthew looked from her to Emma, a watchful expression on his face.

Abruptly, he cleared his throat, then swung Emma into his arms, his eyes looking into those of the little girl.

'Where do you think they've gone, Emma?'

'They're deaded and that's why Auntie Jane and Grandma look after me and Harry.' She studied him pensively. 'You can look after me as well, if you like.'

'I'd like that very much.' Matthew's voice was husky as he carefully put Emma back on the ground. 'But now, you'd better ask Auntie Jane to help you with that dirty face, while I get ready to go back to work.'

'Run along, Emma, I'll be with you in a minute.'

Patting the little girl on her dungaree-clad bottom, Jane ushered her from the room.

'Sorry that you were put in such an embarrassing position.' she began nervously.

'Don't be silly. I'm flattered that Emma feels so comfortable with me after such a short time. I only wish. . .' His voice faded as he took her hand and studied her, his dark eyes unreadable.

'You only wish what?' Nervously, Jane pulled her hand free.

'I don't think that now is the right time to discuss it. But at least knowing about your loss gives me some insight.' He paused. 'Why didn't you tell me before? It explains so much.'

Jane swallowed. 'I'm not the sort of person who tells all as soon as I meet someone. Maybe I can't talk about it, have you thought of that?'

'Come here.'

'Oh.' Jane couldn't prevent a cry of surprise as Matthew seized her arm and drew her towards him; she was even more surprised at his all-embracing hug. A very comforting hug, she had to admit, savouring the sensation of his face close to hers and the clean fresh smell of him.

'I quite understand if you don't want to say anything,' he murmured gently against her cheek, 'but please, if ever you're down and need to talk, remember I'm available. All right? What was it, a road accident?' He held her away and stared deep into her eyes.

Jane merely nodded, unable to say a word for the lump in her throat.

'Well, a broad shoulder is right here if ever you

need it. Now,' he said briskly, glancing at his watch and reaching for the buckle at his waist. 'Unless you want to help me, while I put on clean trousers. . .'

He laughed softly as Jane fled from the room, her cheeks ablaze. Emma might feel comfortable with Matthew, she thought, but I certainly don't. Despite the invitation to cry on his shoulder if need be. And I can't see living in the same house is going to make it any easier. Oh, well, we can only wait and see. Trying to forget Matthew and his unexpected hug, Jane hurried to the bathroom, suddenly aware of the noisy splashes coming from there and anxiously wondering just what Emma was up to.

'That was delicious. I've never tasted better Yorkshire pudding.' With a contented sigh, Matthew sat back and patted his stomach. 'If I continue to have much more of your home cooking, I shall get as big as a house.'

Jane sneaked a glance from the corner of her eye at the way the denim material of Matthew's jeans fitted so snugly. He's certainly not put on weight, she thought. I've never seen a flatter or trimmer stomach.

All her earlier worry about having Matthew to stay had gone, dissolved in his gentle friendliness and the way he'd slotted into their little family as smoothly as though he'd been with them for months rather than just a few days. Admittedly she'd been on duty part of the time, and Matthew himself had come in very late when on call, but having him in the house had added an extra dimension to all their lives and she was dreading the thought of his leaving them.

'I hope you'll still come and see us, even when the workmen have finished with your house.' Muriel Shelby echoed Jane's thoughts, pushing back her chair and gathering the dinner plates together. She slid them into a bowl of water before turning to the fridge. 'I've got ice-cream and some raspberries, if you want.'

'Not for me, thanks, Mum. But I'm sure Matthew will be able to manage some, won't you?' She heard the teasing note in her voice with a mild sense of disbelief. It still astonished her that she should feel so at ease now. Possibly it was because she was on home territory that she could relax in his company, but whatever the reason, it made a pleasant change.

Though she still felt a breathless excitement at the thought of seeing him, felt that she was only half a person until he arrived, she was comfortable in his company in a way she'd never known with anyone else.

'I might manage just a little ice-cream, if you'll both join me.' Banging his spoon on the table in a parody of Harry's favourite noise-making activity, Matthew stared hopefully at mother and daughter. In fact, thought Jane, he looks just like a small boy at the moment; his dark hair was ruffled across his brow, a hint of mischief curling his strong sensual mouth. But the broad shoulders, emphasised by his navy sweater, were anything but boyish and Jane looked away from his penetrating stare, worried that he might read from her expression her yearning to run her hand over the smooth woollen material.

'OK. You've persuaded me,' she grinned.

At her nod, Muriel filled three small glass dishes with chocolate ice-cream, then returned to the table once again.

'Have you got to rush back to the hospital, or are they able to manage without you for just one evening?'

Jane smiled at the disapproval in her mother's voice. In the short time that Matthew had been with them, the older woman had become almost as protective of Matthew's welfare as she was of her grandchildren.

'I'm not working tonight.' Matthew spooned up the last of his ice-cream, stirred busily at his coffee, then leaned back, linking his hands behind his head. 'I think I've done my share for today. We had three emergencies; one wasn't actually a heart attack.' He smiled at Jane. 'You'd have been interested; it was an aortic aneurysm. A man of sixty, never been ill before, terrible chest pain to start with, afterwards the pain radiating into his back. Typical X-ray, with a widening mediastinum.'

'Whoa,' Muriel Shelby protested, 'how about letting me in on the secret?'

'Sorry,' Matthew said apologetically. 'Well, you know the large blood vessel that leads away from the heart, carries blood to all the rest of the body—the aorta?'

Jane's mother nodded. 'It's surprising how much you pick up, even by just living with a nurse.'

'Well, an aneurysm is like a blister in the artery

wall, and with the enormous pressure of all that blood-flow,' he glanced round. 'Sorry, not the best subject for the dinner table.'

'Don't worry,' Jane laughed. 'Mum's got a stomach like iron. Anyway, we've all finished eating.'

'Well, as I was saying, with the pressure that builds up, the bulge in the aorta wall can partly split, so that blood leaks into the abdominal cavity, causing terrible pain, very low blood-pressure with shock and it's potentially a life-threatening condition. Luckily nowadays we can operate, but it wasn't always so.' He sipped his coffee and replaced the cup in the saucer. 'In fact, it was a favourite condition for fiction writers years ago, when people in books had a fatal disease and they never knew when it would kill them.'

'What happened to the patient you saw today?'

'He went to the General. They've got a very good vascular surgery team, and when I enquired he was out of Theatre and doing very well.'

'Is heart trouble becoming more common?' Mrs Shelby asked interestedly.

'I'm afraid so, still the biggest killer in this country and women are becoming more affected. At one time, women were usually susceptible after the menopause, but now it seems to be taking hold of those much younger. Must be the stress of the modern lifestyle, with women spending more time out in the workforce.'

'So there you are, Jane, try and find a good man to take care of you and you'll reduce your risk of heart problems.' Her mother grinned.

'Not if he's the wrong man,' Jane said sharply.

'Surely that has to be more stressful than a career, however pressurised?'

'So you think that all is well if you find the right man?' Matthew stared at her thoughtfully.

'I didn't say that. In fact, I'm just as ambitious as the next person and really enjoy my work,' Jane said coolly, irritated at Matthew's assumption. 'But I know the most stressful situation for me would be marriage to the wrong person.' She ran her hand impatiently through her hair. 'Still, it's not likely to be a problem for many years. My first responsibility is towards Emma and Harry.'

'But surely that doesn't preclude a relationship?' Matthew's voice was bleak.

'Who knows?' Jane shrugged.

'Well, I think you're. . .'

'Er—more coffee, anyone?' Muriel Shelby's calm tones cut in hastily.

'Not for me, thank you.' Matthew got smoothly to his feet, seeming to tower over both women. 'I have to go over to my house and check what progress has been made, if any, but then the rest of the evening is my own.' He turned to Jane, ignoring her earlier impatience. 'Would you like to do something?'

'Eh? Me?' Jane stared at him open-mouthed. 'Such as?'

'Well, go for a drink, or perhaps there's a film you'd like to see?'

Her mind raced feverishly. She couldn't imagine anything she'd like more than to have some time alone with Matthew but. . .

She was increasingly nervous at how important he'd become, increasingly frightened of the fact that she might betray her feelings. For whatever she felt about him, there could be no possible future. Her first priority had to be Emma and Harry and what woman could ask a man to take on other people's children, not even her own, but twice removed, as it were?

'Well,' he laughed. 'Why all the doubt? I promise I'm not planning to abduct you or anything.'

'Go on, love,' her mother urged. 'It'll do you good.'

'If you're sure. . .?'

'Absolutely sure. That's settled, then.' Pushing aside his chair, Matthew moved to the sink and began running hot water into the bowl.

'What are you doing?' Jane stared at him in astonishment.

'Just going to give a hand with the washing-up. There's no harm in that, is there?'

'Mum and I'll see to it. You said you wanted to check on your house. Go on,' she ordered as Matthew stared at her doubtfully.

'Well, I must admit, it would be easier to look round while there is still a bit of daylight left.' He glanced through the window at the gathering dusk. 'But, if I miss my share of the chores this evening, I insist I bring everyone breakfast in bed on Sunday.' He dried his hands and walked towards the door. 'I should be back in about an hour. Have a think about where you'd like to go, in the meantime.'

'Oh, darn it, there's the phone. Excuse me.' Pushing past Matthew, Jane hurried to the hall, her excitement at the thought of Matthew's invitation making her breathless.

'Hello, Jane Shelby.'

'Do you have Matthew Carvalho staying there?' There was something slightly familiar about the voice at the other end of the line, making Jane frown for a moment.

'Yes, he's here. Who's calling?' Her heart sank. Probably the hospital. Couldn't they let him rest for just one evening?

'It's his brother. I'm sorry to trouble you but it is a bit of an emergency.'

'His brother?' Jane blinked. Matthew had never discussed a family with either her mother or herself. Somehow, when she'd wondered about his background, she'd pictured it as being in Portugal. 'Hold on, I'll get him for you.' She hurried back to the kitchen.

'It's for you—your brother.' She smiled nervously. 'He sounds very like you on the phone.'

Trying to stifle her curiosity, Jane moved to the sink and picked up a tea-towel, ignoring Matthew's worried expression as he went to the hall.

'Is there something wrong?' Muriel Shelby's face was sympathetic as she looked at her daughter.

'I don't know. Why do you ask?'

'Just thought you seemed a bit tense.' Her mother splashed noisily at the plates, stacking them on the draining board.

'Jane, I'm afraid we'll have to alter our plans.' Both women turned quickly as Matthew's voice came from behind them. 'My brother's call was to say that my father isn't very well.'

'Oh, I'm sorry.' Jane flung down the towel and moved towards him. 'Nothing serious, is it?'

'Probably not, but because I'm the medical one in the family my mother likes me to be there if anyone is ill.'

'Do they live far? Is it much of a journey?'

'No, only about an hour's drive. If I leave now, I'll be able to get there in good time.' He patted her arm. 'Sorry about this evening. I was looking forward to it.'

Jane felt quite proud of her nonchalant shrug. 'Not to worry. I might have been rather poor company, for I'm pretty tired. An early night will probably be better for me.'

'But it won't be as much fun, surely? Oh, well, I'll try not to wake you when I get back.'

'You won't be staying overnight, then?'

'No, I have to be at the hospital first thing tomorrow.'

'Goodnight, see you later.' But she doubted if Matthew heard her goodnight call. Just as well, she thought, as the closing of the front door sounded a death knell to her happy anticipation of a few minutes ago. I must have sounded like some pathetic waif.

CHAPTER SIX

'HERE are those books I promised. I think you'll find quite a lot of useful stuff in them.'

Jane glanced up from the desk with a smile of thanks. Though she'd greeted Matthew's original suggestion with enthusiasm, she now had doubts as to whether she would have enough mental energy to cope with the study programme he'd outlined. Night duty, with Emma and Harry, made her ever more tired.

But he'd gone to a lot of trouble and it seemed churlish to refuse outright.

Something of how she felt must have shown on her face despite the dim lighting in the ward, where the occasional sigh and groan from the patients broke into their conversation.

'I'm very grateful,' she added hastily. 'I did try to get some of the books from the School of Nursing but, of course, I can only have them for a limited period. And I don't want to buy textbooks if I'm not going to make good use of them. They're so expensive.'

'Still no news about David's will, then? Or rather his lack of one?' Matthew's concern was plain from the way he studied her so intently.

I can't believe how much I've told this man, Jane thought, but it's so easy to confide in him.

'No further progress. The solicitor did allow me

some funds for Emma and Harry, for clothes and so on.'

'I don't suppose you'll let me help.'

Jane stiffened. 'No, thank you,' she said firmly. 'I'm grateful for the offer, but we can manage. The children aren't suffering and though I have to admit finances are a bit tight, never would I consider borrowing from anyone.'

'I'm quite offended. Surely I'm not just anyone? I thought we were friends and what are friends for, except to help one another? Anyway, it would only be a short-term measure.'

'Excuse me, that's Mrs Reynolds' bell.' Hastily, Jane left the desk and went to the bedside of the patient in the far corner. She couldn't tell Matthew the main reason she was unable to accept a loan; he would think her mad to worry about being beholden, to have their lives more intertwined. He'd made it obvious that he thought of them as friends — witness his words just now. But she wanted so much more, and it was getting harder all the time to disguise how she felt.

'Yes, Mrs Reynolds?' Smoothing the duvet over the elderly lady, Jane smiled absently, her thoughts still on Matthew.

'Could I have a drink, please, Nurse?'

'Of course. The hot drinks are on their way, or did you mean squash?' Thrusting aside the turmoil in her mind, Jane hurried to the kitchen and stirred at a cup of hot chocolate. She should be concentrating on her work, not be mooning about like some lovesick teenager.

Walking briskly back to the unit, she set the cup

on Mrs Reynolds' locker, picked up the charts and took them back to the desk.

By the time she'd done so, Sally was alone, sorting through a tangled heap of bright red wool, her face almost the colour of her knitting as she struggled to understand the pattern.

'He's gone,' she muttered, not looking up from her needles but obviously able to sense Jane's searching look.

Jane struggled. 'Well, there's nothing to keep him here, with the unit as quiet as this. If it stays this peaceful, I might get a chance to go through some of these study papers that Matthew brought.'

'Still keen to do the ITU course, then?' Sally glanced up, her knitting resting in a heap on her lap.

'Well, it won't be for ages. I can't possibly work full time, do the course with all the studying that that entails and take care of my two. But I've definitely not given up the idea completely.'

'Good for you. Me, I'm keen to get back on the general ward as soon as I've finished this lot of nights.'

Jane felt her heart sink. She hated the idea of not having Sally's cheerful company at work. The other girl had made the night duty more pleasurable in every way and though Jane had never discussed her feelings, she guessed that Sally, though too sensitive to ask outright, had some idea of how Jane felt.

'Did you see that Cliff Jennings is booked for an angioplasty, by the way?' Sally glanced up as Jane shuffled through the paperwork.

'Oh, no. He hasn't had another MI?'

'No, but his coronary arteries are definitely worse

and the cardiac team want to avoid surgery if at all possible. Apparently, his kidney function isn't all that it should be.'

'I noticed that his urea and creatinine were high, the last time he was admitted.' Jane flicked through the case notes. 'He hasn't a lot going for him, has he? I hope the angioplasty is successful. It's got to be less traumatic having a tiny balloon inflated in the blood vessels, rather than having a full artery replacement.'

Sally was silent as she busily counted stitches, then glanced at her friend.

'I think he'll finish up having a coronary bypass graft and in my humble opinion, if there's any doubt, they ought to get on with it, not put it off any longer.'

'Well, perhaps the powers-that-be hope he'll be fit to go back to work more quickly with just the angioplasty. Especially as he has a young family. And he's such a nice man, so uncomplaining.' Jane pulled a face. 'Must be terrible for his wife. When is he coming in to have it done?'

'I'm not sure — next week some time, I think. If he does have surgery, you ought to ask if you can see the operation.'

'But he wouldn't have it done here, would he?'

'No, but I'm sure that if we asked Matthew he would be able to arrange for you to go to the General and watch.'

Jane wrinkled her nose. 'Don't know if I fancy it, particularly as I know the patient.'

'Rubbish,' Sally said briskly. 'It's interesting if you've never seen any cardiac surgery. I'm not one for working in Theatre, but I thought it was fascinating when I went.'

'They take the long vein from the leg and use it to replace the damaged coronary arteries, don't they?'

'Yes, and it's amazing to see the heart stop beating, once the chest is opened and the bypass machine takes over. I was surprised at how small the heart actually is.'

'About the size of your clenched fist, isn't it? So I was told.'

Sally nodded. 'Only trouble with working in any cardiac or coronary unit,' she giggled. 'Doesn't half take away the romantic idea of the heart. After all, it's no more than a pump.'

'You cynical thing. St Valentine doesn't do much for you, then. . .oh, just a minute, there's one of the monitor alarms.' Swiftly Jane got up from the desk and hurried to the bedside, but was relieved that the emergency was no more than a disconnected lead. Sticking it in place with a fresh electrode on the patient's chest, she gently straightened the duvet over a restless but still sleeping Mrs Reynolds and walked quietly back to her chair.

'All right? Changing the subject, if it stays quiet, instead of studying, why don't you get your head down during your break? It will do you a lot more good than all that reading in the middle of the night.'

'Trouble is, I always feel ten times worse after a sleep,' Jane remarked.

'Well, see how it goes. Oh, blow this.' With an impatient movement, Sally thrust the knitting into her bag and stretched her arms in the air. 'I'll make a drink. Tea or coffee?'

'Let's have real coffee. There's still some left from Mr Brannigan's thank-you parcel.'

'Does that mean I'll have to struggle with the percolator?' Sally grimaced.

'Sit there, I'll get it.' Laughing at her friend's expression, Jane hurried into the small kitchen, filled the kettle and set out mugs, milk and sugar while she waited for the water to boil.

'You lazy devil,' she grinned, thinking of Sally's reluctance. 'I'll be lazy as well,' Jane muttered, 'and just make it in a jug. Save all that washing-up afterwards.'

She filled the jug with hot water, placing it on a narrow shelf while she cleared away some of the cups left behind by the previous shift. I'll have to have a moan at them tomorrow about that, she thought, as she wiped the last two and hung them on the hooks.

Just then the lid of the kettle rattled impatiently and Jane flicked the switch and took hold of the handle. But her hands were still wet from the washing-up and she screamed as the kettle slipped and boiling water shot out in a stream down the front of her right leg.

'What's the matter, what happened?' The door swung back and Sally's frightened face appeared.

'Quick! Ice from the fridge,' Jane said faintly. Her leg felt as though it was going to explode.

'What's going on?' Jane heard the voice of the new arrival as though from a distance.

'Jane's burnt her leg,' Sally muttered, her voice betraying the horror she felt.

Without a word, Matthew pushed Sally aside as

she tried to break ice free from the fridge and lifted Jane in one swift move, sitting her on the draining board as he dragged off her shoes and flung them to the floor. 'Pull up your skirt,' he ordered, turning on the cold tap at full flow and running the water over the front of Jane's leg.

'I'll take care of things here, you get back to the unit.' Matthew nodded to Sally. 'Are you OK? Is the burning any easier?' He turned back to Jane.

'I think so.' She bit her lip, trying desperately not to moan aloud, but despite her efforts at control she couldn't prevent a few tears that escaped and slid gently down her cheek.

'Oh, don't cry, my love.' Matthew gently thumbed the tears from her cheek and hugged her close. 'You can't imagine what it does to me to see you upset.' Through her pain, Jane was amazed to feel Matthew plant a gentle kiss on the top of her head, before returning to the task of splashing more cold water over her burns.

'It feels much easier now,' Jane sniffed, wiping her face with the back of her hand. 'Could I get down?' As the burning subsided, she began to feel slightly ridiculous perched on the side of the sink, her feet and legs partly immersed.

'Leave it a bit longer. We want to cool the area thoroughly then I'll have a look to see what damage you've done. How do you feel in yourself?'

His warm, reassuring voice, his obvious concern brought the threat of tears once again, but Jane swallowed quickly, not wanting to show any sign of weakness in front of Matthew. Gradually the burning sensation subsided, leaving no more than a tingle

in her leg. Carefully, Matthew helped her to the
floor.

'Let's see if we can peel off your tights, but be
careful in case there is any blistering. Though I think
we might have got away with it.'

Too dazed to feel self-conscious, Jane eased off
her soaking wet tights and wriggled her legs free. To
her amazement, apart from some reddening on her
shin and a large blister on the top of her foot,
everything looked almost normal.

'Right, down to Casualty and get a dressing on
that foot. Meantime, I'll go and set Sally's mind at
rest, tell her that you're not mortally wounded.'
Matthew shook his head, wonderingly. 'I don't
know, leave you for five minutes. . .'

'I didn't do it on purpose,' Jane groaned. She
rested on the chair, her injured leg stretched out in
front of her. Now that the immediate tension had
gone, she was feeling more and more self-conscious.
Though there was no need, for Matthew's attitude
had been completely professional. Except for the
moment when she'd started to cry. Had there been
more than just concern in his voice? And had he
really called her 'his love' and kissed her better, so
to speak?

'You must be more careful. How on earth did you
manage to do such a silly thing?' He stopped
abruptly. 'Sorry, I shouldn't carry on like that. I'm
sure you're still feeling shocked. Let's put a covering
on your burn to keep out the air and get some coffee
or tea inside you.'

Not waiting for her to agree, Matthew swept a
protesting Jane into his arms and backed through

the door, taking her into the ward and putting her on the nearest empty bed.

'I don't want to go to A&E,' Jane said firmly. 'I can have just a dry non-stick dressing on it for now and check it again in the morning.'

'I think you ought to report it and go home if necessary,' Sally said doubtfully. Her face was very nearly the same washed-out white as Jane's.

'You both look like ghosts. Sit down, the pair of you, I'll get the coffee and we can decide on the next move once we've had a drink.' Briskly pushing Sally on to a chair, Matthew disappeared in the direction of the kitchen, barely giving her a chance to collect dressings and plaster. By the time he'd returned, Jane's leg was neatly wrapped in gauze and bandage and felt much more comfortable.

'I can't go home. How would you manage if I left?' Vigorously, Jane stirred a second spoonful of sugar into her cup and swallowed the hot coffee gratefully. 'Not only that, it would scare Mum half to death if I suddenly appeared in the middle of the night.'

'I hadn't thought of that,' Sally frowned. 'But you can't carry on working with your leg in that state.'

'Actually, it's stopped hurting now. I'm sure if I take it pretty easy it won't cause me any problems.' Quickly, Jane tucked her hands out of sight, for they still had a tendency to shake. 'Let me have this coffee and then see how I am. Please?'

'All right, but any signs of real discomfort and off you go,' Matthew said firmly. He drained his coffee, putting his head back as he swallowed and showing the powerful column of his throat.

'I'll just make sure our patients are resting.' Sally hurried towards the centre of the unit, leaving an uncomfortable silence behind her. Suddenly, the significance of all that had taken place, how Matthew had held her in his arms, the gentle way he'd comforted her when she'd been so upset, even the unwitting intimacy of the moment when he'd helped her to peel off her tights, stirred like a whirlpool in Jane's thoughts and she fidgeted, uncomfortable at being alone with him.

Which was perhaps silly of her, because lately, particularly since his stay at the Shelby house, there had been a closeness between them that had deepened almost daily.

Now his expression was unreadable in the dim pool of the bedside light, his face a series of shadows that revealed nothing of what he felt. If only, Jane thought, if only. . . Still, what what was the use in wishing? There could never be anything deeper than friendship between them, given her circumstances. Unable to think of a thing to say, Jane moved to the edge of the bed and slowly stood on the floor.

To her relief, apart from a feeling of increased pressure in her foot as she lowered it, there was little pain.

'It doesn't feel too uncomfortable.' She smiled reassuringly at Matthew, who frowned as she walked slowly from the bed towards the desk.

'I'm OK, Sally,' Jane reiterated. 'I'll be all right to stay on duty, honest.'

'Well, I spoke too soon about having a quiet night,' Sally aligned the case notes on the desk, 'and

I can tell you, Jane Shelby, that sort of excitement I can well do without.'

She shook an admonishing finger in her friend's face before hurrying in answer to the impatient sound of a buzzer.

'Hang on a minute.' Matthew moved to the desk and sat beside Jane. 'Where do you think you're going?'

'I'm going to get my tights, dry them out and see about giving Sally a hand.'

'Not before I check to see if your leg is all right. Is it painful?'

Jane shook her head. 'No, the skin just feels a bit taut, as though it's crinkling,' she said graphically.

'In that case we'll leave the dressing as it is.' He bent forward and ran a gentle hand down the length of her shin, and despite her efforts at self-control Jane couldn't prevent a small shiver at his touch.

'Not cold, are you?' Matthew's voice was concerned. 'Could be delayed shock.'

'I'm sure I'll be all right. Thanks for taking such good care of me,' Jane muttered, suddenly shy at all the attention.

Matthew murmured something as she limped to where Sally was busy with Mrs Reynolds.

Jane thought she heard him say, 'I'd like to take care of you always,' but surely she must have misunderstood? Turning as she reached the cubicle, a sparkle of mischief now alight in her green eyes, she smiled back at Matthew, sprawled in the chair.

'What did you say just then?'

'I said. . .' He shook his head. 'Never mind. Now is not the time and the place for a heart-to-heart.

Just put it down to the burblings of a very tired man.' He yawned, showing white, even teeth that were such a contrast to his olive skin. His obvious fatigue gave him a little-boy-lost look that made her draw in her breath with a slight hiss. Somehow, he was even more attractive in his tiredness and she had to control an urge not to hurry back to his side and hug his head to her breast.

'Shall I check the dressing before I go?' Obviously unaware of her thoughts, Matthew yawned again as he stretched his arms above his head.

'No, thanks.' Quickly Jane joined Sally at the bedside, trying not to picture how it would feel to have Matthew's large but gentle hands once again touching her.

By the time she and Sally had settled the elderly lady, and returned to the desk, Matthew had gone, and somehow there was a gaping emptiness as Jane saw the vacant chair.

'Matthew said earlier you ought to report your scald so I've bleeped Medical Sister to let her know. Are you sure you'll be all right to work the rest of the night?'

'Absolutely sure,' Jane said firmly. 'Once I get my tights dry, I shall be back to normal.'

'You're very lucky that Matthew turned up when he did.' Sally pushed her fingers through her hair as she sat at the desk. 'I'm sure his prompt action saved you an awful lot of pain.'

Jane nodded. 'That's so true. Funny how you panic. Even with my nursing, plus I did a first-aid course once, my mind just went blank at the crucial moment.'

'Well, I wasn't much better,' Sally murmured apologetically. 'Instead of fiddling with those stupid ice cubes, I should have put cold water on immediately. Not that I would have been able to lift you up as our hero did.' Sally grinned. 'If you hadn't been in such pain, it would have been funny. Sorry, I'm not being unsympathetic, honest, but you looked as though you were being whirled up on a roller-coaster.' She paused and looked down at the desk. 'What was it like being in his arms, then?'

'I didn't notice, I was too busy trying not to scream,' Jane muttered. 'But he was surprisingly gentle for such a big man.' She chewed thoughtfully at her lower lip. 'He's the sort who always takes over, isn't he? I suppose it's because his working life is constantly dealing with patients *in extremis*.'

'Also, he's very continental at times—have you noticed?' Sally smiled dreamily. 'Lovely old-world manners, always gets up and offers you a chair and stands back for you to go into the room first, that sort of thing.'

Jane looked pensive. 'True enough, but he's also continental enough to think of women as delicate little flowers that need to be protected. Can be very suffocating, especially for a girl who's always had to make her own way and now has extra responsibilities.'

'That's a bit grumpy for someone who's just been treated with such delicacy. I wouldn't mind a bit of tender loving care occasionally.' Sally sighed and stretched her long legs out in front of her.

'Even though the heart is no more than a pump?' Jane teased. She shifted in her chair. Her leg was

definitely feeling almost normal, the only soreness
the blister on her foot. 'Anyway, enough of Matthew
and my boring injury. I'll just check on our two
proper patients.'

'You stay there.' Firmly Sally pushed Jane back.
'I'll go and see what's happening. I want to make
sure Mrs Reynolds hasn't had more abnormal
rhythms. And when Matthew gets back we'd better
ask him if he wants her to have another dose of
digoxin.'

Jane's insides fluttered nervously. Somehow she
didn't really want to be with Matthew again just yet.
She couldn't help wondering if there was any significance in his kiss, was still acutely aware of the feel
of his arms as he lifted her and what she could only
think of as his tenderness as he bathed her scalded
leg. She would have liked a little more time to try to
calm down before seeing him again.

'What time will he be back?'

'He didn't give a time. I think he said he was going
to Cardiology to check on some angiograms that
were done earlier, so I suppose it depends how long
that takes.' Sally paused. 'Are you sure you'll be all
right to work the rest of the night?'

'Positive,' Jane said briskly. She got to her feet
and stacked the mugs and coffee jug on the tray. 'I'll
just go and wash these up, while you go and see to
the. . .'

'You leave well alone, we don't want any more
disasters.' Matthew's voice looming out of the dimly
lit ward nearly made Jane jump out of her skin.
Startled, she swung round and just managed to stop
herself shouting.

'For goodness' sake, please don't keep telling me what to do. I'm very grateful for your first-aid, I know you saved me from a lot of discomfort, but I think I'm quite capable of deciding how much I can manage.'

'I'm sorry if you find my attention so irritating.' Matthew's face was as dark as thunder; his shoulders, hunched in his white coat, seemed to loom over her and she couldn't help but feel apprehensive at his obvious annoyance. And despite her nervousness, she was acutely conscious of the smell of his cologne and his sheer masculinity that seemed to envelop her.

'I'm sorry,' she gulped.

'There's no need to apologise,' Matthew said in silky tones. 'I thought I'd better warn you that I've been interfering again in your affairs. I saw Night Sister as I left Cardiology and she's coming here to sort out an accident report.' He smiled as he spoke, but Jane shivered, for there was no warmth in his expression, just a hint of something she couldn't read. If she didn't know it was very unlikely, she would have thought that Matthew looked deeply hurt.

Sally grimaced and hurried away to the cubicle, ignoring Jane's pleading gaze.

'I'm sorry,' Jane muttered again, but Matthew either didn't hear her or chose to ignore her attempts at apology. Retrieving case notes from the desk, he began to study them as though his life depended on it.

How could I have been so thoughtless and rude? Trying not wince, Jane shifted her injured foot. He

was as kind as could be and I threw his kindness
back in his face. And I can't possibly tell him why.
He'd probably be acutely embarrassed if I told him
that it's all because I want to hide how much he
means to me.

'If I go home now, it will worry Mum to pieces,
and apart from that, I know the hospital is very
short-staffed tonight.'

Matthew replaced the case notes on the desk and
leant towards her. 'No one is indispensable. If Sister
suggests you go home, I'll take you and make
arrangements to collect your car in the morning.
Or——' he raised a warning finger as Jane opened
her mouth to speak '—or,' he repeated, 'if you'd be
happier, you can go and rest in the visitors' bedroom
for the night and we can reassess your burns in the
morning.'

What's the use? Whatever I say, he's going to deal
with it in his own way, Jane thought wearily. She
stretched her bandaged leg out in front of her.

'Did you put some Flamgel on the blister?'

'Yes, sir,' she nodded.

'Good.' Matthew twisted the lamp so that the light
shone directly on to her shin. 'Mmm, that looks
much better.'

'I told you. . .'

'Hello, what's been happening here?' Sister's brisk
tones interrupted Jane.

She knelt on the floor, both she and Matthew
looking intently at Jane's burnt leg.

Makes me feel like an exhibit in a zoo, she thought
grumpily.

'Hmm, it looks as though there is only surface

redness here,' Sister rested a finger gently on Jane's shin, 'and I think we'll leave the dressing on your foot for the time being. I'll send someone to help Sally and you can. . .'

'Jane would rather not go home in the middle of the night.' Quickly Matthew explained Jane's dilemma.

'Right, in that case, you can rest here overnight and we'll see how you are in the morning. Sally, would you take Jane to the visitors' bedroom, please, while I get you some help?'

Quickly she dialled a number and Jane murmured, 'Goodnight' over her shoulder as she left the ward. Clutching her tights and feeling more and more like some inanimate parcel, she walked into the visitors' room.

Well, she told herself, as she peeled off her uniform, stretched out on the bed and pulled the duvet over her shoulders, you've certainly blown any hope of anything developing between you and Matthew after tonight's little effort. You've done really well. If he had any feelings for you before, he's certain to have changed his mind by now, having seen what a grumpy devil you are.

Tears of self-pity oozed slowly down her face. Why did everything she tried to say to Matthew come out wrong? Hastily, she reached for her uniform, found a crumpled tissue in the pocket and scrubbed at her eyes. If he did glance in to say goodnight, there was no way she wanted to be found crying.

She blew noisily into the tissue and stretched out on the hard, unfamiliar bed. What was happening to her? Where was all her assurance, her ability to cope with whatever fate threw her way?

Ever since she'd know Matthew, she'd had such feelings of uncertainty, on the one hand longing to accept his help, his kindness, his way of caring, on the other afraid of how much he was beginning to mean in her life. There was no future for them; there couldn't be, not with Emma and Harry to care for. The sooner she came to terms with that thought, the better it would be for all concerned.

And it was childish of her to read any sort of hope into Matthew's gentle care of her earlier. It was probably no different from how he'd behave to anyone in the circumstances. Even the kiss, she told herself firmly.

Comforted that she'd managed to sort out some of her ideas, Jane punched the pillow into a more comfortable shape. But though her earlier tiredness washed over her in waves, the night was a long, restless one, and in spite of her good intentions a feeling of loss that she didn't fully understand weighed like an undigested meal inside.

CHAPTER SEVEN

'WHAT will we have to do, Auntie Jane?' Emma's eyes, wide with apprehension, gazed at the waiting train at the edge of the platform. Her new-found confidence seemed to have gone astray and she clutched at Jane's hand as though she would never let it go.

Jane flicked on the brake of the pushchair and crouched down so that her face was level with that of her niece.

'It's nothing to be afraid of, pet, honestly. We're going on something like a big bus. You won't mind that, will you?' Doubtfully, Emma shook her head. 'And as soon as Uncle Doctor gets here, we'll be on our way and I promise you, you'll really enjoy it.'

Jane stood and tugged anxiously at her pale green top, tucking it more firmly into the waistband of her cotton trousers as she stared at the few remaining passengers hurrying aboard. She hoped Matthew wouldn't be long. With only two carriages, they could have a problem getting seats.

She breathed deeply, trying to calm her own churning stomach, not noticing the smells of hot metal that blended incongruously with the scent of a brave display of early lilac hanging over the fence-posts at the end of the platform.

Despite the time he'd spent at their house, Jane still didn't feel completely at ease with Matthew.

Not that he'd done anything to make her nervous. It was her own emotions that disturbed her, and the effort it took to disguise how she felt.

'Though I needn't have worried quite so much before he came to stay, as we saw so little of him,' she muttered to herself. 'What with being on call, lectures, plus rounds and research studies, he seemed to be with us only for the occasional meal. Even so, despite being busy, he remembered to send me those lovely flowers.' Her mouth curved softly, as she thought of the cheeky get-well card that had arrived with the small bouquet. He must like her a bit to have bothered, mustn't he?

He'd been excellent company, charming to her mother and herself, and seemed to enjoy being with the children. Now that the repairs to his house were finished, Jane knew his return to his own home would leave a big gap in all their lives. Especially hers.

'I must say, young Emma, he was the perfect house guest.'

'Pardon?'

'Never mind. Just look at Harry, chewing his thumb again. It will be all gone if he carries on like that, won't it?'

'Don't be silly, Auntie.' Emma wriggled in the pushchair, her red trousers wrinkling as she tried to get free. 'Can I get down? It too tight.' Impatiently she tugged at the holding strap.

'Hang on, Uncle Doctor will be here soon.' If he's much later we'll miss the train, Jane fretted. I can't possibly get the pushchair and two children aboard on my own. It's bad enough trying to get them both organised in the car.

She shifted impatiently, a swell of resentment rising inside. Surely Matthew would have got in touch, if he'd been unable to come?

'I don't know why I arranged to meet him here,' she frowned. Anxiously she checked the time both with her watch and the station clock and stared towards the entrance yet again. 'Maybe this day out isn't such a good idea after all.'

'Pardon, Auntie?' Emma's small voice cut into her worried ramblings.

'Nothing important, Emma.' Absently, Jane ruffled her niece's blonde hair, an unexpected belch of engine noise from the diesel making her jump as it filled the station with an oily smell. Suddenly dispirited, Jane turned the pushchair towards the exit.

'Sorry, I'm late.' A tall figure hurtled past the startled ticket collector; Matthew, his leather jacket undone, the front flaps adrift as he ran, skidded to a halt beside them.

'Come on,' he gasped, 'no time for explanations for the moment.'

He pulled Harry free from the pushchair and thrust him into Jane's arms. Then with one swift move, he'd picked up Emma, folded the chair and levered the four of them through the nearest carriage door into a heap on an adjacent seat. They'd hardly sat down before the train started and gradually eased away from the station.

'Here, let's get ourselves comfortable.' Pushing back a lock of hair from his forehead, Matthew shrugged off his jacket, a dark blue T-shirt hugging the breadth of his shoulders and emphasising the colour of his eyes. Gently, he placed Emma beside him on the dusty moquette upright seat, and exhaled, puffing out his cheeks.

'I thought you were going to leave us stranded,' Jane said accusingly. But she couldn't prevent a smile of welcome lighting up her face. 'You look decidedly harassed,' she grinned, unfairly pleased that perhaps for once, Matthew wasn't totally in control.

Anything to hide the way her heart had responded to his appearance and the feeling she had of completeness, once he'd arrived. Again that sensation that she was only half a person without him.

'I'm sorry. There was news of Mr Jennings just as I was about to leave and I had to sort it out there and then.'

'Oh, what's happened?'

'He has to have surgery and I was arranging a bed for him at the General. It must be soon, his condition is worse.'

'Oh, no, poor man,' Jane said, her green eyes widening in distress.

'Am I forgiven?'

'Of course, don't be so silly. I was only worried that the children shouldn't be disappointed.'

'Well, I would hope that you might have been a bit upset as well.' Matthew pulled a face.

'Er — yes.'

He stared at her for a moment, then with an uncharacteristic sigh, looked at the swiftly passing scenery. 'I think we might have a pleasant day.' He hugged Emma close to him. 'What do you think of the train so far?'

''S all right, I suppose.' Emma still looked doubtful, but she'd lost some of her nervousness once Matthew had arrived. He has a marvellous way with them, thought Jane, studying him intently when she thought herself unobserved.

'Have you ever thought of doing Paediatrics?'

Matthew looked at her in surprise. 'Kid's medicine? No, I've always been interested in Cardiology. Why?'

'It's just that you seem to be so fond of children and these two adore you.'

His face lit up in a beaming smile. 'They do?'

'It's obvious. As soon as you got here, Emma immediately felt safe, and when you're around Harry never plays me up the way he does when we're on our own.'

'He obviously likes the masterful touch, a man's strong hand.' Matthew bent close and looked into her eyes. 'Do you like the masterful touch?' he whispered.

Jane fought against the blush that warmed her face and neck. She could see tiny flecks in the deep blue colour of Matthew's eyes and the scent of his aftershave, combined with the essence of his own aroma, filled her nostrils and almost made her giddy. She swallowed hard and turned her head away.

'As a matter of fact, I hate people bossing me about. It comes of being small, I suppose. Everyone thinks they have to take over, and I like to make my own decisions and not rely too much on others.'

'So I've noticed,' Matthew said drily. How's your leg, by the way?'

'Much better, thanks, and thank you again for the flowers.'

'My pleasure entirely.'

'Anyway, tell me more about Cliff Jennings.'

'There's not a lot more to tell. They tried to clear the blockage of his arteries with the balloon, as you know.'

Jane nodded.

'Well, apparently it wasn't successful, and though I hate to hand over one of my patients I'm afraid his only answer seems to be surgery. He'll be having a bypass graft some time next week.'

'Any chance I could see the operation?'

'Certainly. I'll have a word with the cardiac surgeon, James Blair, and organise it for you if you like.'

Jane sank back against the seat. 'I know I shouldn't get involved with patients, but there's always one that's a bit special, isn't there? I think it's because he has a young family and if anything happened and they were left without a father. . .' She was suddenly aware of Emma's apprehensive stare. 'Enough said. Emma, look at those cows, they're all facing the same way.'

'Why are they looking at that tree over there?' Emma tapped impatiently at Matthew's arm.

'Do you know, I'm not sure?'

He continued talking quietly to Emma and once again Jane was struck at how quickly he seemed to be able to soothe Emma's worries. It was easy to forget at times just how much the little girl understood of what was said. And talk of fathers not being around. . . Not the best subject to discuss in Emma's hearing.

'Thank goodness, Harry's quiet,' murmured Jane as the train clattered on its way. 'That cloth book is a treasure; despite all his efforts, it's still in one piece. Now that he's learned to crawl, anything that keeps him still for more than a few minutes is a godsend.'

'You really love these two, don't you?' Matthew studied her intently. 'Whatever your circumstances, you wouldn't want to give them up.'

'Of course I wouldn't.' Fiercely, Jane hugged Harry to her. 'What do you mean?'

'Never mind.' Matthew turned to Emma, pointing at the countryside skimming past.

What was Matthew suggesting? Give up the children? Jane frowned and stared from the window. She barely noticed the villages of Cotswold stone nestled in the dips of the sweeping countryside, nor the newly ploughed fields with a dusting of fresh green shoots that laid a delicate carpet of colour; a dark green bus, struggling up a steep country lane, blurred then disappeared like something in a dream.

But Jane saw little, as she worried at Matthew's words and what he'd been trying to say.

'Penny for 'em.' Matthew gave her a sidelong glance.

'Oh, nothing worth a penny,' she protested, afraid he might guess what she was thinking.

'I'm sure your thoughts must have been worth something. You were miles away.'

'Just that it's nice not to have to worry about anything for once, that's all.'

'Must have been a tough time for you and your mother.' The sympathy in his voice almost undid her composure.

'Well, it's not a situation I'd want to experience again in a hurry, I must admit. Anyway,' Jane said briskly, suddenly conscious of Emma watching yet again, 'no sad thoughts. We're off to have a good time, and I for one intend to enjoy myself.'

'I'm already doing that. In fact, I always enjoy myself in your company. . . Ugh, Harry, you little beast, take those sticky fingers away from my ear.'

Suddenly, Emma giggled at the expression of disgust on Matthew's face and Jane found herself joining in. Soon all three were laughing together, as Matthew pulled Harry's clutching hand away from his neck.

'I'm sorry, Harry can't stop dribbling at the moment; he's teething like mad.' Jane spluttered helplessly.

'Don't apologise. It was worth all the discomfort if it made you laugh like that,' Matthew murmured softly. 'I think that's the first time I've really seen you laugh properly.'

'I'm normally quite a happy person.'

'Of course. It's just that life has been pretty tough, hasn't it?'

Jane nodded, not speaking. She knew why she'd found it so easy to laugh. It was because, despite all her efforts at remaining detached, she felt a lightness of spirit whenever she was in Matthew's company. And, in spite of her being careful, her feelings were developing into something stronger, something to frighten her with their implications.

A sharp squeal of surprise dragged Jane from her thoughts, thoughts that were running on dangerous lines.

'What is it?' she muttered to Emma, blinking as the brightness of the sun appeared to follow the train on its slow but steady journey.

'I saw some horses running.'

'I thought something awful had happened. Come on, let's get you tidy; we'll soon be there.' She was careful not to look directly at Matthew, nervous that the sparkle in her eyes, the readiness of her smile might betray her.

Hastily she gathered Harry to her, wiping his face with a damp tissue, despite his protests as he wriggled, almost landing on the floor.

'Here, let me have him.' Matthew's strong arms took the struggling baby from her as Jane tidied a more amenable Emma.

'What did you think of all the horses and cows, Emma?'

But Emma was too absorbed in the sights outside the window to answer, holding out one hand then the other towards her aunt in an absent-minded fashion as the train drew slowly into the little station.

Curiously, Jane stared round as they clambered on to the platform. 'I didn't even know this station still existed,' she said, eyebrows raised.

'Ah, so I am able to provide a few surprises, then,' Matthew teased. He soon had the pushchair unfolded with Harry strapped in, turning it on its back wheels as he ushered them all towards the exit.

'Where are we going?' Emma scuffed her feet unwillingly, swinging her brightly coloured bag in her free hand.

'It's all up to Uncle Doctor,' Jane said, hurriedly shifting the responsibility and delighted when she saw that for one second Matthew was lost for words.

There was no one to take their tickets, in fact by the time they left the station was deserted, but, outside, a small bus, its diesel engine squelching impatiently, was ready to leave.

'Come on, that's our bus.' Hastily Matthew ushered them ahead, hoisting the two children and pushchair inside.

'This is a regular mystery tour,' Jane gasped as she sank back on to the plastic-covered seat.

'Have faith.' Matthew patted her arm and it seemed a very short journey before he was shepherding them together yet again as the bus halted with a squeal of brakes.

'Thanks a lot.' They waved to the smiling driver and watched the bus depart; Jane stared round curiously as they waited at the roadside.

'Is that where we're going?' She pointed to an impressive stone-pillared entrance, the drive lined with horse-chestnut trees leading from it through smoothly grassed land.

Matthew nodded. 'Yes. Melton Manor. There's a children's playground, a picnic area, and if our two aren't tired we might even manage a look at the house as well.'

'Our two'. The words seemed to echo in the air as, taking Emma's hand, Jane followed Matthew past black wrought iron gates to the sweep of gravel drive that brought them to a Georgian manor house. The white-painted front gleamed in the spring sunshine; windows set square on either side reflected the sun's rays with splashes of orange light.

'It looks like an Impressionist painting, everything vivid and sparkling clean,' Jane muttered admiringly.

'Have you not been here before?'

'No, never. I've heard of it, of course. It's funny, isn't it, you never seem to visit places that are close to home?'

'True. I'm the same when I'm in Oporto, in Portugal.'

'But that's not actually your home, is it? I thought your family lived in England?'

'They do, but Oporto is my second home. Lots of my family are involved in the wine and port trade there. We'll go and visit them one day.' He paused, waiting to see Jane's reaction to his words.

'That would be lovely,' Jane murmured breathlessly.

'But that's for the future. Today, we're visiting Melton Manor.'

With Emma's warm little hand clasped in her own, Jane studied the house as they approached, enjoying its balanced lines and the smooth lawns that sloped gently from the front. Clumps of late daffodils were scattered like yellow exclamation marks among the greenery.

It didn't take them long to walk to the rear of the house, where an area of woodland had been converted to an adventure playground.

'Look, Emma, another train, much smaller this

time.' Emma stared, obviously impressed at the miniature railway, the train's whistle accompanied by the shrieks of its young passengers.

'The slides and swings suitable for the smaller children are on the far side. Shall we go over there?' Matthew pointed through the trees.

But Emma needed no invitation, already running eagerly to where a gaily painted slide, with a complement of carefully watching mothers, was situated. But she stopped abruptly, as several children pushed their way to the front.

'Come along, Emma.' Gently Matthew encouraged her forward, watching carefully as she joined in enthusiastically. With a grateful sigh, Jane sank back on to one of the wooden benches, spreading a rug on the ground for Harry.

The intermittent chirring from the many dovecotes that surrounded the Manor provided a soothing accompaniment to the shouts of the children and the short bursts of sound from the train as it appeared at intervals. The occasional sounds seemed to enhance rather than spoil the air of peace that emanated from the surrounding woods and parkland.

'It's amazing, I've lived around here for years and hardly knew this place existed.' She turned as Matthew settled beside her on the seat. 'What made you think of coming here?'

'It's one of my favourite places. I hope you get to like it as well.' He was staring straight ahead, not looking at her, but Jane was acutely aware of everything about him, the sensation of his body beside her, the powerful thighs resting easily on the seat. His bare arm in the short-sleeved T-shirt was so close to hers it felt as though the separate hairs of each were entwined.

Carefully, she studied the strong profile. He wasn't what she would call a conventionally handsome man, though his eyes would have graced any film star, but even when his face was in repose, as now, there was a lift to the corner of his mouth and an air of kindness that showed in every line of his face.

What did it matter, if sometimes he seemed high-handed? She knew his actions only stemmed from kindness and perhaps she was too sensitive, being small and desperately keen to show she could manage as well as anyone.

'I don't understand why you were so abrupt that first time we met?' Unbidden, the words came out as she thought back to their first meeting.

He turned to face her and grinned disarmingly.

'I thought you were some kid trying to vandalise my car. I'd only recently had the paintwork done after it had been scratched along one side and the thought of it happening again was enough to get me going.'

'I'd been for an interview; I was looking very smart that day, not like 'some kid',' Jane said huffily.

'I know you were, but once you'd put on that red woolly hat, and with your being not very tall, I had a definite impression you were much younger. Anyway I'm sorry if I frightened you. Apology accepted?'

'Of course, and I wasn't frightened, just angry that someone could be so. . .' She paused.

'Bossy? Arrogant? Jumping to conclusions?' With

every question, Matthew moved closer to her, and Jane could feel his breath softly caressing her face.

'Auntie Jane, Uncle Doctor, look at me!' The squeal dragged Jane's attention hastily back to her charges and she gasped as she caught sight of Emma.

'What are you doing?' she shouted, for Emma had taken the opportunity when neither Jane nor Matthew was watching to climb to the top of a large helter-skelter. Completely unafraid, Emma waved, her outline swaying in for a moment before she copied the boy in front and lay face-down on the mat, swooping round the curves so quickly, she was a blur. Unable to move, Jane watched aghast as Matthew raced to the slide and swung a laughing, excited Emma into his arms.

I should be concentrating on the children, not. . . not gazing at Matthew. . . Her legs like jelly, her voice barely audible, Jane seized the little girl by the arm and hauled her close. 'Don't you ever do anything like that again. You are not to go anywhere — anywhere, do you understand? — without asking me first. You could have fallen. . .' She blinked angrily at the tears that threatened as an image of Emma's broken body came into her mind.

'There was no harm done,' Matthew murmured softly.

'I know, but there so easily could have been. If you hadn't been so quick off the mark. . .' Unable to continue speaking, she stretched up and hugged Matthew to her. 'Thanks,' she whispered.

'Hey, my pleasure and privilege. No need to get so upset.' He put a finger under her chin and gently lifted it, so that their faces were only inches apart.

'It was almost worth the shock of seeing Emma at the top of the slide to have a hug from you.'

Hastily, Jane sat back, frightened that she'd nearly betrayed herself. Matthew looked into her eyes, not speaking for a moment, then cleared his throat. 'No shouting at Emma,' he said quietly, 'she's only three years old. . .'

'Quite,' Jane countered sharply. 'And I'm at fault for not being more watchful.'

'Don't be too hard on yourself; anyone can make a mistake. It mustn't spoil our day.'

Jane glanced down at her niece, noticing with a pang the anxious frown on the little face staring up at her.

We couldn't be more upset if we were Emma's parents, she thought. The picture of Matthew and herself as a couple pushed aside her anger over Emma. Of course the whole idea was ridiculous, but ridiculous or not, the thought, once it had taken root, wouldn't go away. Hugging Emma to her, Jane apologised to her niece, then turned to Matthew.

'It was my fault, but I won't go on about it.' Jane got to her feet and stood with her hands behind her, looking not much older than her charges.

'We were both a bit remiss.' Not giving Jane time to catch her breath, Matthew leant forward and kissed her soundly on the cheek. 'Come on, let's go and feed the ducks, they've got all sorts here and then we can think about tea. How about an ice-cream for everyone?'

The rest of the afternoon passed like a dream, though Jane made sure she watched the children meticulously. Now that Harry had learned to crawl, he had a tendency to lose patience at being confined to the chair, so they took time to rest beside the lake, where mallards, snow-white Aylesburys and a pair of stately swans hovered, waiting to be fed.

'Look at those greedy little birds.' Matthew set Emma in front of him as a pair of coots, their feet skittering frantically across the surface of the water, skidded to a halt, scooping up the pieces of bread as fast as Matthew threw them.

'Isn't this beautiful?' Jane stared at the parkland, the sweeps of grass dotted with copses of poplar and blackthorn, a cascade of daffodils in front of the house which was just visible from the lakeside, the stone terrace set with weatherbeaten urns and a waterfall, the drops sparkling in the spring sunshine.

'It is, isn't it? I'm glad I've had the chance to show it to you.' Matthew smiled at her warmly.

'Do you want to walk a bit further?' They wandered slowly along the path, Matthew holding Emma firmly by the hand. There were few other visitors and Jane let her imagination stray, picturing the house and grounds as they must have been in the past.

At times she was afloat on a cloud of happiness, delighting in Matthew's presence and his obvious enjoyment of the children; at other times she found herself studying him intently, trying to decide where their relationship was going.

Were his feelings for her getting any stronger? Or was he just a very kind man who had nothing much to do during a lovely spring day and thought he might as well fill it with their company? It still surprised her that he wasn't married and she had to admit to herself stirrings of curiosity about a previous relationship he'd mentioned. But he'd never referred to it again and she was too uncertain to question him about his past.

They reached another play area and Emma, not at all disturbed by her adventure on the helter-skelter, raced happily with a little boy of about her own age, while Harry, delighted to be free of the pushchair, crawled busily on the grass, occasionally trying to stand, his small sticky fingers clinging tightly to her trousers. Watching the children, Jane was immersed in a peace that she hadn't known since Penny and David's deaths.

'It's a pity Mum couldn't have come with us.' Jane spoke idly, but as she said the words she wished them gone. For Matthew turned those piercing eyes in her direction, seeming to read her every thought.

'She would have been more than welcome, you know that. But I thought she wasn't. . .'

'Oh, she couldn't make it today. Her arthritis has been playing up.'

'It's a shame. She would have enjoyed herself here, I'm sure.'

Jane flushed as she remembered her mother's words when the invitation from Matthew arrived. Far from her joints being more painful, with the coming of the warmer spring weather Mrs Shelby had felt much better. But she'd been adamant that she wouldn't intrude on the outing.

'I'm pretty sure that it's your company that Matthew wants,' she'd said firmly, pushing aside Jane's protests.

'Chance would be a fine thing,' Jane had said with a wry smile. 'You're forgetting the children.'

'That's as maybe, but I've seen the way he looks at you.' Her mother had nodded knowingly and returned to the kitchen.

The vivid memory of the implications in her mother's words brought a flush to Jane's cheek and she turned away. If only, she thought. If only.

'Come on.' Seizing her hand, Matthew pulled her to her feet and Jane couldn't prevent a laugh as she stumbled against him. She closed her eyes, the sensation stirred by Matthew's body almost overwhelming. Pull yourself together, she told herself sharply, and stop thinking like some lovesick schoolgirl.

Abruptly, Matthew released her hand. Was it her imagination or had his breathing quickened as he'd held her near?

'Pack up the bags,' he said crisply, as he scooped Harry from the rug, firmly removing a strand of grass that was disappearing rapidly into the little boy's mouth. 'I've another surprise for you.'

Not stopping to explain, he swept the little group ahead of him towards the back entrance of the house. There were even fewer people here, where a high gate led through to a brick-walled garden, the quiet only disturbed by one or two early bees among the blossom that lined the walls and added their perfume to air.

'Where are we going?' Jane puffed, hurrying to keep up with Matthew's long strides. 'Isn't this the private part of the house?' She glanced over her shoulder, expecting at any moment that an irate gardener or member of the household staff would appear and ask them what they were doing.

'Trust me.' Without another word of explanation, Matthew ushered them through a wooden door, which hung askew on its hinges and protested with a screech that could have come straight from a horror film.

Holding tightly to Emma's hand, Jane followed almost on tiptoe, the sensation of trespass growing with every step they took.

Suddenly ahead of them, in the thinly carpeted hallway, a door swung back and Jane paused, waiting for a reprimand.

The man who appeared, with dark red hair and dressed, despite the warmth of the afternoon, in a tweed jacket and jodhpurs that had seen better days, didn't demand to know where they were heading. Instead, he grinned widely, holding out a hand in welcome as they went towards him.

'Matthew, great to see you. I didn't realise it was today you were coming to visit. Why didn't you let me know?' He stared curiously at Jane and the two children, and Jane was acutely conscious of the state of her trousers, grass stains on the knees and a streak of Harry's drink on the front of her shirt. Hastily wiping her sticky palm down the side of her leg, she took the man's outstretched hand as Matthew introduced them.

'This is my brother, Stewart. I'm sure if we ask him nicely he'll be able to offer us some tea. Won't you, Stewart?'

'Do you actually live here?' Jane had stared wide-eyed at the galleried hall, the dark polished wood of the staircase, the pictures that covered the faded silk paper on the walls.

'I do.' Stewart nodded towards his brother. 'We all knew that Matthew would have to go into some sort of caring position, but when we were kids he wasn't sure if it would be with people or animals. He was always fascinated by birds with broken wings, stray dogs, anything that needed help. Eventually, he decided on medicine, but I've stayed with the family business, running the house and some wine importing as well.'

'And what about your parents?'

'They've got a bungalow not far from the estate. My father still helps part-time.'

'Is he better now?' She turned to Matthew, trying to disguise how her spirits had fallen at Stewart's words about Matthew being always one for strays, for those needing help. Perhaps that was how he regarded her, in which case her growing hope of a deeper relationship was a vain one.

'Oh, he's fine, thank you.' Matthew grinned and took her arm.

'You might have warned me,' Jane hissed later, when she and Matthew had a moment alone.

'Don't be so defensive. Stewart loves to have visitors and I checked before we came that it would be all right to bring you all.'

'That's as maybe,' Jane muttered, 'but if I'd known I was expected at the manor, I would have worn something more suitable.'

'Don't be silly, Stewart isn't about to judge someone by their clothes. Anyway, you look fine.' He tapped her lightly on the cheek with his forefinger.

* * *

Once she'd recovered from the shock of her surroundings, Jane was able to relax, and to her surprise thoroughly enjoyed herself. In the large kitchen, where a bright red Aga took the chill from the high-ceilinged room, she sat at the table and watched as Stewart poured boiling water into the teapot, stirred it busily and sat once again at the wooden kitchen table.

'How's the world of heart attacks?'

'Busy, of course. As Jane can tell you.'

'Very true. Oh, thank you.' She took the cup and saucer from Stewart and set it in front of her. 'Are you sure Emma and Harry won't be too much trouble for Mrs Whitfield?' The housekeeper had seized both children as soon as they'd finished their drinks and carried them off, Jane didn't know where.

'Yes, they'll be fine. She's taken them to the old nursery so they'll have a lot of fun with the rocking horse and train set.' Matthew bit into a scone and chewed hungrily.

'So you work with Matthew, do you?'

'Yes, I suppose you could say that.' Jane sipped at her cup, frowning over the rim. She was bewildered at the visit, wondering if there was some point to it that she didn't understand, but it was difficult. . .

'I work nights so that I can be at home with Emma and Harry,' she explained as both Matthew and Stewart said little, busy with the sandwiches, fruit cake and scones.

'I know.' Stewart nodded approvingly. 'I've heard all about you. All the family has been very keen to meet you.'

'Oh, what has Matthew been saying, then?'

'He's told us. . .'

'I think it must be nearly time to make a move,'
Matthew broke in hastily, wiping his mouth with a
napkin as he got to his feet.

'But you've only just got here.' Stewart seemed as
bewildered as Jane felt at the sudden end to the
pleasant tea-party.

'I know, but I expect Jane is keen to get the
children home; they must be tired by now.'

And like a whirlwind he picked up their bags,
called a hasty goodbye to his brother and set off up
the staircase at a run, swiftly reappearing with a
small child under each arm.

CHAPTER EIGHT

HASTILY, Jane replaced her cup on the kitchen table, trying hard to ignore the rattle it made in the saucer. She'd been feeling increasingly weary, and had had what she thought of as a 'funny turn' once before when very tired, but had pressed on, hoping it would go away.

Perhaps her body was trying to tell her it was time she had a rest, but with being so short-staffed at work she couldn't consider time off at the moment.

She chewed half-heartedly at her toast, not sure if the discomfort in her stomach was due to hunger or indigestion, but determined to finish eating despite her lack of appetite.

It's not surprising I'm finding life a bit much, she grimaced. Still, as long as Mum doesn't find out.

'Do you want your shower now or before you go to work?' Her mother's voice broke into her thoughts and quickly Jane forced a smile to her face.

'I'll have it in a minute, thanks.' Wearily, she pushed herself up from the table. 'Do you want a hand?'

'You,' Muriel said sharply, pointing in Jane's direction, 'go and relax for five minutes. You're like a ghost, all pale and wan. I can manage the meal.'

'At least now that David's insurance is going through we can have that holiday,' Jane said, pretending an enthusiasm she was too tired to feel.

Moving sluggishly to the living-room, she stretched out on the settee, unnerved by the unusually silent house. Emma had gone to a friend's birthday tea and Harry was having a prolonged nap, so she could with an easy conscience take the weight off her feet.

'Blast the phone. All right, I'll get it,' Jane called. She still did all she could to save her mother effort though in fact Mrs Shelby's arthritis had improved during the past two months. Their GP had been unable to offer any good reason except to suggest that the extra responsibilities had in fact led to a remission in the symptoms. Sighing, Jane picked up the receiver.

'Hello, Jane Shelby.'

The sound of Matthew's deep voice at the other end of the line acted on her like a powerful drug. Her heart beat faster, her expression lightened and as she glanced at her reflection in the hall stand mirror she saw a smile that had been missing for too long.

'I've just got back and thought I would ring to see how you are. Not too tired after the day out?' His trace of accent was more pronounced on the telephone, making her suddenly shy.

'We're all fine,' she said brightly. 'How about you?' Jane shook her head in disbelief. How can I possibly feel so different from how I was ten minutes ago, solely because Matthew has phoned?

'Have you recovered from your burn? Your legs aren't a problem?'

'No more than they've always been,' Jane laughed. 'They're still the size of sparrows' legs.'

Ruefully she stared at her lower limbs stretched out in front of her as she perched on the bottom stair.

'What nonsense, you're perfectly proportioned.'

'Thank you, kind sir; small but beautifully formed, is that it?' Laughter bubbled into her voice, her joy at hearing from Matthew, combined with his obvious concern, pushing aside all her earlier depression. She'd not had the chance to ask him why he'd been in such a hurry to leave his brother during their day out, but right now she didn't care. It was enough that he'd got in touch.

'It's good to hear you laugh.' Matthew's voice was suddenly sober. 'You don't laugh nearly enough.'

'I'm sorry I'm such a misery.'

'No, you're not.' His voice was firm. 'The reason I rang, apart from asking how you were, is to find out if you and the children would fancy another trip?'

'Matthew, it's very kind of you, but you mustn't feel that every free moment you have should be spent with my family.'

'Why not? I enjoy it.'

'Surely you would rather be with someone else for a change?' Why doesn't he ask me out on my own? she wondered, stifling a whisper of disappointment. Apart from the one occasion, when the call to his father had put paid to their plans, Matthew had made no attempt to ask her out again on her own. Perhaps Emma and Harry were the real attraction.

'You'll make a wonderful father one day,' she said softly.

'Thank you. Something to look forward to. In the

meantime, please may I share your two? As long as I'm not in the way.' His voice was suddenly anxious.

'Who is it?' her mother whispered, poking her head round the door.

'Matthew,' Jane muttered, placing her hand firmly over the mouthpiece of the phone.

'Ask him if he'd like to come to supper.'

'Matthew, just a minute, Mum's just asking if you might like to come to supper one night.'

'I'd love to. But we'll take the children out first and give her a quiet afternoon.'

What about giving me a quiet afternoon? Jane thought, with a rueful grimace. But her conscience thrust aside the idea as soon as it rose from the recesses of her mind. Dearly though she loved the children, it really would be nice if just once Matthew asked her out, treated her as a woman in her own right, not just as an appendage to the children. Nice! It would be heaven, an intimate dinner for two, a stroll home through the evening air. . .

'I must go.' Matthew's voice broke into her reverie. 'I'll see you later. You are working tonight, aren't you?'

'Yes, thanks for ringing.'

Returning to the kitchen, Jane put her cup and plate on the draining board before going upstairs. Though she was still tired, it was amazing how a simple phone call from Matthew, plus the knowledge that she would see him that evening, even if only at work, perked up her spirits so much.

Whistling softly through her teeth, Jane padded into the bathroom, and swiftly peeled off her outsize T-shirt. Tunelessly, she hummed as she soaped herself under the shower, staring at her body as if for the first time. Covered with suds and perfumed with the light flowery scent of the shower gel, it really looked as though she at last had stopped losing weight. Though never in a million years could she be called curvaceous, both her hips and bust seemed more shapely. Small but beautifully formed, she laughed to herself, spluttering as soapy water went into her mouth.

'Who am I kidding?' Briskly, she rubbed herself dry and walked into her bedroom, the towel wrapped around like a sarong.

Pausing only to slip on bra and pants, a pair of denim shorts and a peppermint-green T-shirt, which brought out the colour of her eyes, Jane slid her feet into sandals and hurried downstairs and out through the front door.

The warmth of the early summer sunshine was a benison to her skin, making her aware of all sorts of sensations that she couldn't define. A group of warring sparrows squabbled noisily in a patch of dust at the kerbside and the heady perfume from next door's full-blown lilac filled Jane's nostrils.

'Just going to pick up Emma,' she called, waving to her mother, who was in the front garden, chatting to their neighbour.

Enjoying the feel of the sun on her face, Jane walked briskly. It wasn't far to Emma's friend's house, less distance than the walk to the nursery, and avoiding the steep hill, thank goodness. Though the fresh air would do them both good.

'Had a nice time?' Jane stared fondly at her little

niece trotting beside her, a crayoning book and pencils clutched firmly in her hand.

'Mmm,' Emma nodded. 'We had a magic man, who made things disappear.'

'And too much tea, no doubt.'

'Mmm,' Emma murmured again. 'Auntie Jane, when is my birthday?'

'Not long now. Why, do you want a magic man to come to your party?'

'No, I just want you and Granny and Harry, I s'pose, and ——' the little girl paused and took a deep breath ' — and Uncle Doctor.'

'Well, of course, if you want him to come, we'll ask him.'

'Good.' Happily, Emma skipped the last few yards to their gate.

Uncle Doctor, eh? thought Jane, following her niece along the path. Another female fallen victim to Matthew's charms. Even Mum thinks he's the best thing since sliced bread. Oh, well, at least I know I'm in good company.

'Mum, Mum, we're here.' Flinging back the front door, Jane and Emma went through to their small back garden, Jane halting abruptly as she heard the ting of the telephone being replaced.

'There you are, Jane, I've just heard from the insurance office.' Taking her granddaughter's hand, Muriel Shelby ushered them into the kitchen.

'There isn't a problem, is there?' Jane frowned, putting Emma's present on the kitchen table.

'Far from it. Apparently, David's firm has a blanket insurance which provides cover for the dependants of all their employees. Because Penny. . .' Mrs

Shelby swallowed a moment and Jane leant across and gently squeezed her hand. 'Because Penny was killed at the same time as David, it took longer for the details of the policy to be sorted out. Anyway, it looks as though we've got enough money to be going on with and if you want to you could give up nights, even stop working altogether for the time being, at least until we get everything settled.'

Jane stared at her mother.

'But I like working. . .' she began.

'Oh, I know you do, love, but I thought that perhaps you could take on something a bit easier.'

Lost in thought, Jane sat at the table. Give up her job and not have the opportunity to work with Matthew? The idea didn't bear thinking of. Although it was wonderful news that the children would be so well provided for. . . Clearing her throat, Jane looked hard at her mother.

'I think I'm quite happy to carry on as we are at present.'

'But. . .'

'Don't worry so, Mum.' She grinned and flexed her arm. 'Look at that. I'm very strong for my size and we've just established a routine that seems to suit Emma and Harry. More changes could upset them again.'

'But I thought you had your heart set on doing the course. We might be able to find a way to get that organised.'

'That was before. . .'

'All right, we'll see what happens, shall we? Mr Branton, the insurance manager, said to get in touch if we have any problems, but it certainly looks as though finances will be a lot easier, which has to be a good thing.' Muriel Shelby picked up an armful of clean clothes and went through to the hall.

'Well, miss,' Jane sat Emma on the wooden seat, 'that puts a different complexion on matters, I must say.' She took a bottle from the fridge and watched as the creamy milk arced into the blue plastic beaker.

'Don't like milk.' Emma closed her lips in a firm line.

'All right.' Her eyes twinkling, Jane put the milk back in the fridge.

'Well, perhaps I drink some.' Emma quickly changed her mind as she realised there was not going to be an argument.

'Contrary Mary,' Jane teased as she handed back the milk and sank on to the kitchen stool, her elbows resting on the edge of the table, her expression thoughtful. If she gave up her job, she'd have much more time for Emma and Harry, of course. Absently, she leant forward and ruffled Emma's blonde hair.

But I would hate to lose the day-to-day, or, rather, night-to-night contact with Matthew. That's the only sure way I have of seeing him. And as I can't expect anything more, I'm not about to miss out on that.

'Jane—ah, there you are.' The door swung back and her mother appeared.

'You look a bit flushed,' Jane observed absently.

Not answering, Muriel Shelby filled the kettle, plugged it in, then sat at the table beside her daughter. 'What do you think, love?'

'About what?'

'The possibility of not working nights.'

'I think we should carry on in the same way.'

'I worry that night duty is too much for you.'

'I can cope. But it would be a good idea to spend some of the money on a holiday.'

'I couldn't agree more.' Jane's mother poured boiling water into the pot, set out cups and saucers and fetched milk from the fridge. 'Tea for you?'

Jane nodded. 'I can't quite understand why the company didn't contact us before. After all it's been nearly three months since Penny and David's accident.'

'The company explained. From what I can make out, cover is normally provided for the wife. As Penny was involved as well, it made things much more complicated.'

Jane grinned as she stirred sugar into her tea. 'Just think, no more money worries. We won't know ourselves. Not that we've gone short of anything.'

'First priority is a holiday, but it won't be much of a rest with our two.' Her mother refilled both cups and passed one to Jane. 'And you're sure that you're quite happy with things as they are?'

'Quite sure, Mum, so quit worrying. I've even got some study papers, so I can make a start on those soon. It will give me a bit of an advantage if I do get on the course. I told you that Matthew had sorted out some case papers for me, didn't I?'

'No, you didn't, but it doesn't surprise me. He's very thoughtful, isn't he? Where has he got to, by the way? He hasn't been to see us for some time.'

'He's been away, but has asked us out at the

weekend. That was why he phoned earlier. And you must come with us this time.'

'Well, we'll see. I know you don't like to leave me on my own, but, really, it's no bad thing to have a rest from those two imps, much as I enjoy their company.' Muriel Shelby cleared away the tray and ran cold water on to the potatoes in the sink. 'Having said that, you know I'll always take care of them if you want to go out with Matthew on your own.'

'Thanks, Mum, but he hasn't actually asked me, of late,' Jane said drily.

They mulled over their changed circumstances through their meal and Jane found herself still planning various treats for Emma and Harry as she got them ready for bed. A holiday, somewhere like Devon, a really good party for Emma — she sobered suddenly as the reason for the money came to mind. Still, she knew that Penny and David would have wanted things to be as straightforward as possible for her and her mother.

She went quickly to the kitchen but as usual her mother had cleared everything away.

'I said I would help you, but if you're sure you don't want a hand, I must get changed or I'll never be ready for work. Sally is giving me a lift. Now that we've got the extra cash, I might be able to afford to have that new gearbox. I hate being beholden to anyone.'

'You don't have to tell me. Fiercely independent and always have been. All you ever said when you were little was "Me do it myself".' Her mother smiled fondly as she finished tidying the kitchen.

'I can manage the housework.' Her mother held out her hands. 'Look, much better, as you can see.'

'Even so. . .'

'Even so nothing. You carry on with the job, I'll see to the domestic chores. Makes me feel I'm pulling my weight.'

Jane was barely ready, just tying the laces in her black uniform shoes, when the bell sounded. Seizing her bag, she hurried downstairs, called out a quick goodnight to her mother and opened the front door.

'What are you doing here?' Jane gaped in surprise at Matthew's unexpected appearance.

He laughed delightedly at the startled look she gave him. How dear he is, Jane thought, feasting her eyes on his casually dressed figure, registering the snugly fitting jeans, the crisp striped shirt, the scent of his aftershave.

'Hey, I didn't intend to be that much of a shock.' Leaning forward, Matthew peered into her eyes. 'Now, you may not believe this, but I wondered if you might need a lift.'

'I already have one arranged. Sally's picking me up.' Jane frowned. 'How did you know my car was out of action, anyway?'

'I saw it at the garage when I called in for petrol, asked where the owner was and they explained that it was in for repair.' He grinned. 'Pretty sharp of me, eh?'

'Sorry to disappoint you, Sherlock Holmes, but Sally should be here at any moment.'

Matthew shrugged. 'Fair enough. In that case, I'll just pop in and say hello to your mother, if she's not too busy.'

'I'm sure she'll be delighted with the company, but no arranging subtle little plans for me,' Jane warned.

'As if I would. Jane. . .' He paused, gently brushing the back of his hand down the length of her cheek and trailing it across her mouth. Jane tensed, seized with an almost overwhelming desire to kiss the tips of Matthew's fingers. As if he read her mind, Matthew stared at her, then slowly bent forward, his lips following in the wake of his touch.

His mouth was warm and sweet on hers; the sensation travelled through her, a sensation compounded of smell, taste and touch, and she heard herself sigh as she returned his kiss.

'Jane. Oh, Jane.' There was a wealth of emotion in the simple use of her name and she stretched her face towards him, her eyes closed, her mouth soft and inviting.

Gently he kissed her closed eyes, her cheek, each corner of her mouth, the very gentleness of his caresses setting her skin on fire.

'Jane, I've got to talk to you,' he murmured huskily. 'I don't think I can go on. . .'

But the sound of a peremptory beep from the roadside startled her into awareness and, with a muttered apology, Jane pulled herself free from Matthew's embrace and ran to her waiting friend.

'Wasn't that Matthew I saw?' Sally put the car into gear, peered over her shoulder and carefully pulled away from the kerb as soon as Jane had her seatbelt fastened.

'Yes, it was. Is there any reason why it shouldn't be?' How much had Sally seen?

'Hey, don't bite my head off. If you don't want to talk about your love-life, it's no skin off my nose.' Tossing her head, Sally accelerated and the little hatchback shot forward towards the dual carriageway.

'I'm afraid he's nothing to do with my love-life,' Jane muttered despondently. But oh, how I wish he were, her errant heart murmured. Tentatively, she drew a finger around the shape of her mouth, surprised at just how sensual his feather-light touch had been.

'Let's start again, shall we?' Sally sighed as the little car swung through the hospital gates and headed towards the car park. 'I promise I won't poke my nose in where it's not wanted if you promise not to get nasty at any mention of Matthew's name.'

'I'm never nasty. . .'

'There you go,' Sally said warningly. Then she giggled loudly. 'Honestly, to hear us two, you'd think I was insulting you, not paying you the compliment of suggesting that the most devastating man in the hospital is interested in you. Don't say a word,' she continued, swinging her bag on to her shoulder and locking the car door. 'His name shall not pass my lips at all during the rest of the night. Come on, race you to the main door.' She set off at a run, leaving Jane to trail behind her.

Before this evening, she'd never thought that Matthew was interested in her 'in that way'. The words shone in her mind like neon lights. He certainly had shown the greatest kindness towards her and the family, but there had never been more than friendliness in his attitude, never a hint of any stronger feelings.

Until that unexpected kiss earlier. And what had he been about to say, when they were interrupted?

How can I stay casual, she thought, when every time I see him I love him more? There, I've admitted it, even if only to myself. Every time I see him, hear his voice or even think about him, my heart starts its nonsense.

'You're supposed to repair hearts, not break them,' she muttered, looking at the darkening sky as she hurried after her friend. But whatever your feelings about me, Matthew, dear Matthew, I'm not going to give the smallest hint unless and until you say something first.

Jane sniffed at the familiar smells as she hurried through the doors of the ward. All her previous resentment about work had gone; it was difficult to know if it was because of Matthew's influence or because of the easing of the family money worries.

Even the hustle of getting a patient ready for cardioversion as soon as they'd taken report wasn't enough to fluster Jane.

'You know what to do, don't you?' Moving swiftly towards the equipment-room, Sally patted Jane on the shoulder, muttering a mischievous, 'Not a word,' as she hurried past. Rapidly, Jane went over the procedure in her mind. The patient would be anaesthetised, then, when unconscious, would be given shocks from the defibrillator, to settle the rhythm of his heart. It was necessary sometimes, when the usual drugs didn't. She set a trolley with syringes, containing a sedative and muscle relaxant, and a laryngoscope to act as a guide for the tube that would be passed into the patient's throat.

As she steered the old-fashioned ventilator towards the bed, in case it should be needed, a familiar figure in a white coat came into the unit. Taking a deep breath, Jane waved a greeting, hoping she hadn't betrayed her nervousness at Matthew's appearance.

Hastily plugging in the machine, she connected the corrugated tubing in place.

'We're going to put you to sleep for a little while, then treat that heartbeat of yours. The drugs haven't worked as we hoped, so we'll try a small electric current.' Reassuringly, Matthew smiled as he took hold of Mr Rowland's hand. Apprehensively, the elderly man watched until the injection had him drifting off to sleep then Mike, the anaesthetist, passed a tube into his throat, tying it neatly in place with a length of tape.

Gently, he peeled back Mr Rowland's eyelids and studied the eyes intently. 'He's all ready for you, Matthew.'

'Right.' Slipping off his coat and rolling up the sleeves of his blue striped shirt, Matthew pulled the defibrillator into line with the bed, and pressed the switch to charge it.

'Despite all his cardiac drugs, Mr Rowland is still having a lot of atrial fibrillation and the best thing now is to give him an electric shock; very often that will set the heart into a more normal rhythm,' Matthew explained. 'I'll start at a hundred joules.'

Jane watched, fascinated, as the machine hummed

into life, the wave-form of their patient's heartbeat
clear on its soft green screen.

Matthew lifted the two paddles and glanced once
more at Mike. 'Ready? Right, stand back every-
body, away from the bed. Don't want the wrong one
to have a shock.' He placed the discs on their
greased pads, on Jim Rowland's chest, pressed the
switches on each, and the sleeping man's back
arched in response to the electric current that flowed
through his body. The monitor line was briefly
straight, then quickly reverted to a zig-zag that to
Jane's absorbed gaze seemed almost normal.

'That looks pretty good to me.' Mike nodded
approvingly.

'I don't think I'll need to repeat it.' Matthew
stowed the paddles back on the machine and
watched the steady rise and fall of Jim's chest,
counting the pulse at the wrist.

As Jane tidied the bed area, then stowed the
machine in the equipment-room, her thoughts
returned again to Matthew's kiss. Did he perhaps—
could he perhaps. . .? She couldn't finish the question, for her whole body was swamped with sensation that made her breathless. I must forget it for
the time being, or I'll be needing an electric shock
myself. But deep down she knew that being with
Matthew was all she needed. All she would ever
need, if it were at all possible.

CHAPTER NINE

JANE stared at the table with a feeling of awe, noting the gold-tipped cutlery, the fine crystal that reflected the glow of the candles set at intervals along the length of the polished wood, the whole scene framed by deep rose-coloured curtains that were open to the soft night sky, a sky of dark blue velvet, stitched with tiny stars that sparkled like sequins.

She still felt dazed at the realisation that she was actually in Portugal, in Oporto, staying with Matthew's cousin. Paul and his wife had been so welcoming that Jane's doubts about accepting the invitation soon disappeared. She'd even managed to stop worrying over the fact that Matthew was unable to be with them, Emma, Harry and herself, until later.

'Don't know what happened to the caravan in Devon,' she told the empty room. 'Don't know how I was persuaded to come here at all. Hope Mum isn't too lonely without us. Still, the rest will do her good.' Jane smiled, a contented smile. So far, every-thing about the holiday had been wonderful, and both children had settled so well, Jane hàdn't had a moment's concern during their week's stay.

She wandered slowly round Paul and Maria's large dining-room, breathing deeply as perfume from a jasmine bush wafted in through the open window and mingled with the delicious smells of food that drifted from the door at the rear. Suddenly her stomach growled with hunger. Though she'd had more lunch than she normally ate, today the ubiquitous grilled sardines and some *vinho verde*, the lateness of the evening dinner meant that she came to the table with what was for her an enormous appetite.

She was pleased that she was first down; it gave her a chance to have a look round and also time to gather herself together, so it was with a feeling of irritation that she heard the door leading from the main hall open behind her.

'Matthew!' She couldn't control her cry of delight as she saw the beloved figure walk towards her. He studied her for several seconds, not saying a word, the expression of his dark eyes hidden by the line of his lashes. Then suddenly he swept her into his arms and hugged her close, pressing a smoothly shaven cheek to her face, his fresh clean smell making her senses spin.

'Hey, put me down!' Jane said faintly, struggling as she was whirled off her feet. 'I didn't know you'd be here today; Maria thought. . .'

'Shh.' Matthew set her back on the floor and laid a gentle finger on her mouth. 'Just be quiet for a minute while I take a good look at you.' Dark blue eyes stared into cool green ones. 'Mmm, you look marvellous.'

'I feel marvellous,' Jane laughed. 'Your cousins have been so kind, I couldn't have been better cared for. But what about you? How did you manage to get away from the conference? I thought it was on for another week?'

'Come and sit down.' Taking her by the arm, Matthew led Jane to a small curved settee on the far side of the dining-table. 'Let me get you a drink. What would you like?'

'A white port, please.' Now that she'd had time to recover from the shock of seeing Matthew so unexpectedly, Jane felt smothered in shyness and had to swallow in an effort to speak.

'Ah, I'm glad you've taken up one of the local customs.' Matthew moved to a carved sideboard and took glasses and a bottle from inside. 'There's nothing to beat a good white port as an aperitif. Here you are. Cheers.'

Jane took the glass, trembling as her fingers brushed against Matthew's. She was astonished, not to say a little scared, at the depth of feeling the sight of his dear face had aroused. How she loved him! And being with his cousins, staying in his country, seeing places that must be familiar to him, had brought a heightened awareness of how much Matthew had come to mean to her. But she was totally unprepared for the need she felt to reach out and touch him, to rest a hand on his powerful arm as she spoke, to know again the sensation of being held close.

Now she stared with barely concealed longing. He was formally dressed in a charcoal-grey suit, his crisp white shirt and pale silk tie emphasising his tan, and when he smiled, white teeth flashing, her heart somersaulted so severely she could scarcely get her breath.

'You look very nice. I think I've already said that.' He rested his hands on her shoulders, then slid them

gently down her bare arms, gazing steadily as Jane
shivered before pulling away.

She blushed and smoothed down the almond-
green material of her skirt. When she'd dressed
earlier, the length had seemed perfectly acceptable,
but now, with Matthew's warm gaze on her, she
wondered if perhaps she was showing too much leg?

'I told Maria I hadn't anything very grand to wear,
and she said not to worry, it's just an informal family
evening.' Jane gestured towards the table, turning
Matthew's attention away from herself. 'If this is an
informal evening, I'd hate to have to cope when
Paul and Maria are putting on a show!'

'Don't worry. It really is just family and a few
friends.' He swivelled on the seat and stared at her
over the top of his glass. 'It's probably the cutlery
that makes it look so extravagant. That's been in the
family for ages—originally from Brazil, I believe.
Anyway, enough of that. Tell me all that you've
been doing in the past week. And how are Emma
and Harry, of course? We mustn't forget them.'

'They're fine.' Jane smiled fondly. 'Emma can
already say "Bom dia" and "Obrigado". How she
makes the housekeeper understand her, I'll never
know, but she and Angelina get on like a house on
fire. And Harry can swim. Well, doggy-paddle, with
his arm-bands on.'

'And what about you?' Matthew said softly. 'Are
you feeling better for the rest?'

'Oh, your family has been so kind.' Jane paused
and stared at the floor, tracing the zig-zag shapes of
the wood blocks with the toe of her sandal. She
wasn't sure she could stay cool and collected, if

Matthew continued to look at her in that unnerving fashion.

'I've been to Oporto — sorry, Porto — shopping, I've been to visit the Wine Shippers' lodges,' she gabbled, 'had a day at the coast at Espinho; other than that I've been very lazy, just eating and resting and swimming.' She stopped, suddenly aware that Matthew hadn't said anything for some time.

'Anyway, how about your conference?' She dared to look up. 'It was about the different effects of high density lipids and low density lipids, wasn't it?'

'Among other things. Anyway, let's forget work.' He smiled slowly and leaned towards her. 'Jane, I can't begin to tell you how glad I am that we're alone. Dearly as I love Emma and Harry, there's something. . .'

'Ah, here you are.' The light from the candles flickered as the door swung open and Paul's cheery voice echoed behind them. 'We wondered where you'd got to, Matthew. I see you have found Jane and have drinks. Good.' He moved swiftly to the cupboard and took out a glass. 'Do you want another? Our guests will be here soon, but we have time for one more if you wish.'

'Not for me.' Hastily, Jane shielded the top of her glass with her hand, cursing softly under her breath. What had Matthew been about to say, when Paul had burst into the room? Fond though she'd become of her host, at the moment she could have wished him anywhere but on the seat beside herself and Matthew.

Anyway, whatever she felt, she had to make the best of it. Leaning back, she watched the play of expression on Matthew's face as he and his cousin chatted, not really listening to what was said, content to know that Matthew was near.

By the time the other guests arrived, both Matthew and Paul had caught up with family gossip, discussed the vagaries of the port trade and decided that Jane should spend all her holidays in Portugal; without consulting her, she noticed. But during her visit she'd seen how Paul would organise everything for Maria. Somehow it didn't seem to matter, for it was obviously done with such love that Maria accepted most, if not all of Paul's suggestions.

Perhaps if Jane herself knew that Matthew loved her she wouldn't feel she had to constantly prove her independence? Chance would be a fine thing, she thought, giving a wry grin. Maybe the wish of the man to hold the reins was a family trait or perhaps common to continentals, as she'd originally supposed. But it was too much to hope that Matthew's interest stemmed from love. It would need a saint to take on a ready-made family such as she had to offer, and Matthew, kind though he was, couldn't be called a saint.

She suddenly realised the cousins were watching her as she sat, lost in thought. Quickly, she straightened in her chair and smiled at them both, hoping her expresions hadn't given any indication of her thoughts.

The evening's events soon developed a dream-like quality, as she was introduced to Paul and Maria's friends then took her place at the table next to Matthew. In fact, Jane wouldn't have been at all surprised to have woken in her own bed, with the rush to get ready for work ahead of her.

'Is this how Paul and Maria usually entertain? It's very different from our little house.' Jane finished the last of her soup, and set her spoon at the edge of the dish.

'Your hospitality was just as welcoming. Don't put yourself down.' Sternly, Matthew tapped Jane on the nose with his forefinger. He seemed in a light-hearted mood, laughing readily at the jokes of the guests, hugging her to him, translating if there was anything she didn't understand.

'I don't know if I can manage to eat all that.' Jane stared at the next course, a large helping of cod and buttery almonds filling her plate.

'Try a little, I think you'll like it,' Matthew encouraged, picking up a forkful and holding it to her mouth. 'We eat a lot of fish in Portugal, especially *sardinhas* and cod.' He grinned mischievously as Jane chewed.

'It's delicious.' But then anything would be delicious if fed to her by Matthew, she thought, revelling in his attention. 'What's so amusing?'

'I don't know if I should tell you this, but in Portugal it is the man of the house who gets to serve the *bacalhau*. An indication of who is the boss. That wouldn't suit you, would it, with the way you hate to have anyone take charge?' He laughed aloud as Jane punched lightly at his arm, attracting the attention of not only Paul and Maria, but the half a dozen guests as well.

'What's the joke, Matthew?' Paul stared curiously at his cousin.

'Jane's bullying me.' Matthew pretended to shrink in his chair, bringing a rosy glow of embarrassment to Jane's face.

'He's been making fun of me. Matthew, stop it,' she hissed. It was all very well for him to tease her, but she felt as though her cheeks would burst into flame if he carried on. What with the wine and the thrill of having Matthew with her and so full of fun. . .

'I can't believe that he would dare,' a middle-aged man across the table muttered, smiling broadly. 'I saw that punch. What did you say to bring on such an attack, Matthew?'

The man's wife, diamond earrings sparkling in the candlelight, shushed him gently.

'Don't interfere.'

They were all so friendly! Or was she seeing everything through rose-tinted glasses, because of Matthew? Jane couldn't tell, but the rest of the meal passed like a dream, conversation going back and forth, food and more wine appearing, until by the time she'd finished her crème caramel she felt she would burst.

The voices drifted into the background, reaching her only as a buzz of sound until suddenly, unawares, she found her head resting on Matthew's broad shoulder. He stared down at her, his dark gaze intense, a curve to his sensual mouth as she forced her eyes open in an effort to keep awake.

'I'm sorry,' she whispered, 'but I'm absolutely shattered. I think the wine must have caught up with me. Would you think me terribly rude if I went on to bed?' She could have wept with disappointment at having to leave early. But here she was, not drunk of course, but fit for nothing but bed.

'I'll see you upstairs,' Matthew said softly. He pulled back her chair and helped her to her feet.

'Jane's very tired. I'll just. . .'

'There's no need for you to be disturbed,' Jane protested, but Matthew ignored her, a supporting arm in her back as he ushered her through the door.

She barely heard the chorus of 'Goodnights' that followed them. Sleepy though she was, she was acutely aware of Matthew's closeness, of the texture of his sleeve against her arm, of the scent of his aftershave as he held her steady, and a strong desire which she could barely control swept over her, so that she desperately wanted to hold him and bury her face in his chest.

'Sorry.' She smiled, her expression like a sleepy owl. 'I can manage now.' They paused at the foot of the stairs and Jane turned to him.

'Please, don't come upstairs with me. Go back to the others. I'll be fine.' She stood on the second stair, her face now at a level with his, and leant forward, planting a noisy kiss on that mouth so temptingly near.

At the touch of his lips, Jane sobered immediately, her head cleared of its fuzziness to be replaced with a tingling that swept through her, making every nerve throb.

Instead of stepping back, Matthew put a hand behind her head and pulled her close. The second kiss was ice and fire combined, so that Jane was suffused in warmth, but also felt a shiver as though cold water had run down her spine.

'Are you cold?' Matthew whispered huskily, his face so near that his breath blended with hers in a sigh.

'No, not cold,' she gulped. 'Just had a little too much wine, I think.' Whatever had possessed her to kiss him? She must be drunk, but not from imbibing too freely; the presence of this man whom she loved so deeply was enough to make her giddy. But despite the tenderness of his embrace, she still had no real idea how he felt about her.

'You'd better go to bed. I wouldn't want to take advantage of you when you're not completely yourself.'

'But you're not taking. . .' she began.

'No arguments; if you're sure you can manage, I'll see you in the morning.' Gently he kissed the corner of her mouth then went back to the dining-room.

'Damn, damn, damn! I've blown it again, trying to cover my options by implying I was drunk. Just in case Matthew rejected me. And of course, he's too much of a gentleman to take advantage of someone not in their right mind.' She stamped up the stairs, the hollow taps of her sandals an echo of the empty feeling in her heart. Flinging back her bedroom door, she tore off her dress and slipped into a bathrobe, tying the belt with a vicious tug.

With poor grace, her head muzzy again, this time with the effect of Matthew's kiss, Jane tiptoed to the children's bedroom.

Harry was fast asleep, his small legs spreadeagled like a wishbone, one hand tightly clutching his toy rabbit.

But Emma was another story. 'What's the matter,

have you had a nasty dream?' The little girl's breathing was harsh and even in the dim glow of the night light, Jane could see the flush on Emma's rounded cheeks. Swiftly, she placed a hand on Emma's forehead and withdrew it sharply. Her niece's skin was burning hot.

'I got tummy ache.' Jane had to bend low to hear the whispered words and she reached out anxiously as Emma started threshing around in the bed. 'I feel sick.'

Running to the bathroom, Jane seized a bowl and hurried to the bedside. She was only just in time, as Emma noisily brought up her supper.

'Have you been feeling sick for a long time?'

'Long ages. I want Mummy,' Emma whimpered. Jane's heart sank but she managed to stay calm, picking Emma from the bed and sitting with her on her lap.

'Mummy can't be here, but you've got Auntie Jane to take care of you, there's nothing to worry about.'

After wriggling for a moment, Emma seemed to accept her aunt's words and settled her head on Jane's shoulder.

Before long, Emma dozed, twitching at intervals, her skin burning hot to the touch. Jane's arm gradually became numb, but when she tried to put Emma back in her bed the little girl moaned and seized Jane's hand. By the time her niece finally slept and Jane had laid her gently on the bed, she wasn't sure how much time had passed but it had been long enough to cause an agonising cramp in her arm.

Stretching and releasing her fingers, she crept to

the door and waited, holding her breath. She had just edged her way through, when a rattling noise from the bed brought her swiftly back into the room.

'Emma!' Jane gasped at the sight of the little girl, limbs twitching, her breath rasping in her throat.

'Oh, God, what do I do now?' For several long seconds, Jane froze in panic, before she hurried to the bathroom and returned with a bowl of tepid water. It must be a form of heat exhaustion, Jane thought frantically, as she hastily removed Emma's pyjamas and squeezed out a flannel, sweeping the damp cloth down the length of Emma's body. She continued, returning at intervals to fetch more water, until it seemed her whole world had narrowed into a small circle of light which shone on heated limbs and a flushed face. She was so immersed in her task, she didn't hear the door open behind her and the deep voice made her jump.

'What's the matter?' Matthew whispered. 'I heard movement in here and thought one of the children was. . .'

Jane wasn't able to answer as he studied the scene.

'I don't know. . .' She swallowed, unable to continue for the lump in her throat. She mustn't cry, mustn't, but she thought she'd never felt more frightened and alone than in the previous half-hour. Her relief at company, any company, was so great she nearly threw her arms around Matthew's neck.

'You're doing exactly the right thing,' he reassured her. 'I expect young madam has had a bit too much sun. I'm sure it isn't anything worse than that. And cooling her is what she needs.' Taking the cloth from Jane's unresisting hand, he carefully felt Emma's skin, now sprinkled with drops of water that draped the fevered body like tiny pearls. Gradually, her shaking stopped, and soon Emma's breathing became softer in tone.

'She's been having rigors and I was so scared,' Jane gulped. Now that the worst of the crisis was fading, she felt as though she herself had been through a wringer.

'Why on earth didn't you call someone?' Matthew pulled a sheet up over Emma, then, gripping Jane's hands, helped her to her feet. 'If you didn't want to call me, you could have fetched Maria or Angelina.'

'I would have called you, but I don't know where your bedroom is.' Moving wearily, Jane went to the small bedside chair and flung herself into it, not looking at Matthew but aware that he had pulled off his tie and undone the button at the neck of his shirt.

'Could you repeat that?' he muttered in tones of disbelief as he stretched his length on the floor beside her, his head resting against the edge of Emma's bed. 'You would have called on me for help?' Even in the dim light of the room, Jane could see the exaggerated lift of his eyebrows.

'Please, Matthew don't be sarcastic. I know I've been a pain in the way I've behaved at times, but I had my reasons.' She leant back against the small cushion, and closed her eyes. 'I may not have shown it very well, but I do appreciate all you've done for me. No girl had a better friend.' She reached out and took hold of Emma's hand. 'It's just that your brother said you couldn't resist any stray dog, any

bird with a broken wing, and I don't like being in
that category.'

'"There's none so blind as those who won't see".'
Matthew's voice was harsh. 'What makes you think
you're a stray bird?'

'Stray *dogs*, birds with broken wings,' Jane corrected faintly. 'What else am I supposed to think?
Anyway, no arguing, please. I'm too tired to talk
sensibly about anything.'

'I've never thought of you in that way. The only
reason. . . Do you still miss your sister?' he asked
abruptly.

Jane smiled sadly. 'Of course I do. But I have to
get on with my life.'

'And you don't see your life changing at all?'
Matthew spoke so quietly she barely heard the
words; overcome with fatigue, she couldn't be bothered to move, but she sat up abruptly as she felt
Matthew edge towards her.

'Well, eventually. . . What are you doing?' she
whispered. He'd taken her free hand and held it,
kissing the soft skin of her palm.

'Shall I read your fortune?' He peered intently at
her hand and began to speak in slow, solemn tones,
which made Jane giggle despite being so tired.

'Stop it, idiot, that tickles.' She tried to pull her
hand away but he clasped it firmly, the mischievous
smile leaving his face.

'I can see great changes here. Mm, and the usual
dark stranger. Well, not exactly a stranger. How
would that be for a start?'

'I don't know about fortune-tellers,' Jane whispered, suddenly breathless. 'I'd rather not know. . .'

Her voice trailed away as she stared down at him, overcome by a longing to run her fingers through the thick dark hair that fell forward across his brow. Carefully, she slid her other hand free from Emma's loosening fingers and rested it on Matthew's head. The small movement as she pulled away was enough to disturb her niece.

'Auntie Jane, don't leave me.'

Swiftly, Jane stood and leaned across the bed.

'It's all right, darling, I'm here. Are you feeling better now?' Sleepily Emma nodded, seized Jane's hand once more and drifted into a doze.

'Jane, don't leave me,' she thought she heard Matthew murmur, but she wasn't to know for sure, at least for the present.

With a sigh that echoed her own, he released her hand, then got up from the floor in one easy movement and turned as he reached the door.

'I'd better not say any more at the moment. I don't want to risk disturbing Emma, though I'm sure she'll be all right now, but call me if you need me. Otherwise, I'll see you in the morning.' Kissing the tips of his fingers in Jane's direction, he walked silently from the room.

'Blast!' What had Matthew been about to say? Beneath the teasing, he'd given an impression of wanting to talk seriously. But how could he when they never had time alone? Oh, well, what was to be would be.

Hurrying briefly to her own bedroom, Jane collected pillows and a quilt, then returned and set out a makeshift bed on the floor. However much she longed to know what Matthew had been about to

say, her first priority was her niece and she might as
well make the best of the rest of the night.

Plumping the pillows into shape, Jane stretched
out beneath the quilt and tried to empty her mind of
the evening's happenings, though she had little hope
of sleep. But, exhausted by the varying emotions
she'd gone through, she, like Emma, drifted into a
doze. And instead of feeling disturbed by the presence of Matthew in her dreams, she was amazed at
just how rested she felt, when fingers of morning
sunlight crept round the curtain edge.

'How is the invalid this morning?' There was a gentle
tap as Matthew walked through the bedroom door.

Hastily, Jane scrambled to her feet, aware of her
crumpled clothes and creases in her face from the
pressure of the pillow. Blast! He would catch her
before she'd had time to gather her wits together.

Carefully, she rested her hand on her sleeping
niece's face. It was cool to the touch and even as she
stood at the bedside, Emma slowly opened her eyes
and smiled sweetly at the two of them.

'Feeling all right, poppet?' Gently Matthew took
Emma's hand.

'Yes, I'm all better now,' the little girl said matter-
of-factly, her hair a golden mass as she sat up against
the pillows.

'That's good. Fancy some breakfast?'

Emma nodded, reaching down the bed to seize
her teddy bear. 'Teddy is sick this morning, so I
better look after him.'

'You go and get dressed while I take care of these

two,' Matthew suggested, and Jane, relieved at her niece's recovery, slipped away to her own room.

Gathering fresh clothes from the cupboard, she glanced from the window at the vivid blue of the sky which foretold another lovely day. A lovely day that lifted her mood. Quickly, she showered and dressed in cotton trousers and crisp white shirt.

'I've got an outing planned for just the two of us,' Matthew announced, pulling Harry's high chair close to the big wooden table in the kitchen. With just the four of them at breakfast, Jane could picture them as she increasingly did these days, as one family. Too good to be true, for in spite of Matthew's warm friendship she didn't dare to hope that what he felt for her could approach the depths of her love. Still, the family image was wonderful and lit her face with a dreamy smile.

'Hey, wake up.' Matthew broke into her reverie.

'What's the outing?' Jane glanced shyly at him, as she spooned cereal into an eager Harry and buttered toast fingers for Emma's boiled egg.

'Angelina will take care of the children. You can have a break.'

'But the whole holiday is a break. Anyway, hasn't Angelina got enough to do already, with the care of the house?' Jane protested.

'She volunteered; she loves to get them to herself,' Matthew said firmly.

It was true, Jane thought, the housekeeper did seem to spend her every spare moment with Emma and Harry.

Jane grinned, a tremor of excitement running

through her as the idea took hold. 'Where are we going?'

Matthew tapped the side of his nose. 'Wait and see.'

He drained the last of his coffee and stood up from the table, tucking his shirt more firmly into the waistband of his dark grey trousers.

'I'll meet you outside in—what shall we say?—about half an hour?'

Jane nodded happily.

By the time she'd organised the care of Emma and Harry, rushed to her room to change her shirt for a more feminine one and made several nervous visits to the bathroom, the half-hour had more than passed and Matthew was sitting at the wheel of a small red sports car, his dark hair shining like the blue-black feathers of a bird's wing in the sun's glow.

'Sorry, I hope I haven't kept you waiting.' Breathlessly, Jane climbed in beside Matthew, not giving him time to open the car door, and settled back against the cool leather of the seat.

'I have a call to make at the local clinic before we go. Is that all right?'

'Fine, I'm all yours. I mean. . .' Conscious of the double meaning in her unwitting remark, Jane stared intently at the roadside, watching an old man, his skin like leather, perched on top of a cartload of vegetables; the horse between the shafts looked as tired as the driver, she thought.

But Matthew didn't seem to hear anything untoward. He nodded towards the old man as he gunned the engine and drove smoothly from the white-painted villa on to a broad avenue, lined with

almond trees that had shed most of their delicate
blossom to cover the road with a drift of pink.

'I didn't picture Oporto as being this busy before
I came.' Jane stared at the seething traffic as they
drove, cars and lorries hooting impatiently, a con-
stant weave of vehicles forming different patterns
along the broad dual carriageway.

'It's the second city of Portugal, and has a lot of
industry. Plus of course the port trade and, nowadays, the export of *vinho verde*. But we won't be
going into the centre; the clinic isn't far and then
we'll be seeing a much pleasanter part of the
country.'

Shortly afterwards, they drove into a broad
avenue, very like the one they'd left, but here the
trees were covered with acid-green leaves, dappling
the road with patchy sunlight. The clinic, a long low
building, with red-painted signs indicating the wards,
was set in a flower-filled garden.

'It looks more like a hotel than a clinic,' Jane
observed as Matthew parked the car in a tarmac-
surfaced area and hurried to help her alight, tucking
a leather briefcase under his arm.

'It is for the rich.' Matthew shrugged apologetically, leading the way through double swing
doors into a short corridor, with rooms set on either
side.

'This is the coronary care unit here. Very different
from St Adhelm's. I have to see a colleague, with
some papers, only for a few minutes. Would you
like to wait at the nurses' station? Ines speaks
English.' He pointed to a dark-haired nurse in white

tunic and trousers sat at a desk with a central console.

Jane smiled as Matthew introduced her to the dark-eyed girl before he hurried along the corridor, disappearing through a white-painted doorway at the rear.

'You are from England and work with Dr Carvalho?' Ines smiled.

'Yes, I'm a staff nurse in Coronary Care.' Jane perched on the edge of the wooden chair, surprised at how lost she felt with Matthew gone.

'Would you like to look round?' The nurse's brightly lipsticked mouth smiled reassuringly as she gestured towards the door just across the corridor.

'Please, if it's not too much trouble.' Quickly, Jane got to her feet and followed as Ines tapped on the partly opened door and stood back to let her go inside.

The room, a slatted venetian blind covering the window, was fitted with every comfort, and the monitor above the bed, she saw, was one of the latest models.

'Senhor Manuel, this is a nurse from England.'

Jane shook the outstretched hand of the elderly man, as she glanced around the room.

'He has had an attack — the infarct, I think you say — and had damage to. . .to the right ventricle, so there is failure.'

'Your English is very good,' Jane said admiringly. 'I can barely say thank you in Portuguese.'

'I worked for a little time in London. Is that where you live?' She led Jane from the room and into a modern treatment area, with, Jane was interested to see, facilities for fitting pacemakers and an up-to-date X-ray machine.

'I'm from another part of England, nowhere near London,' Jane explained. She gestured at the different equipment. 'It's beautifully fitted out here. Is coronary disease very prevalent in Portugal?'

'Pardon?' Ines frowned uncertainly.

'Do you have many cases?'

'Not so many as in England, but I think like most countries it gets worse now.'

They chatted easily, discussing the contrasting styles of different specialists, the ones eager for surgery to deal with heart disease, the others with a more conservative approach.

'Dr Carvalho, he likes to take things more slowly, not rush in, doesn't he?' Ines moved to the nurses' station and pushed a chair in Jane's direction, perching herself on the edge of the desk.

'You know him, then?' Jane asked eagerly.

'Yes, he work here for some time. He is a very good specialist, always thoughtful of the patients and the staff.' Her voice was warm as she talked about Matthew, a barely concealed glow in the dark brown eyes.

'And do you find. . .?' began Jane eagerly, anxious not to miss the chance to learn more about Matthew.

'Ah, there you are.' Jane cursed under her breath at the sound of Matthew's voice as he appeared in the doorway. Goodness knew what she might have discovered about Matthew if the conversation had gone on a bit longer. Though she shouldn't really be eager to gossip about the man she loved.

'Ready to go? Thank you, Ines.' He nodded and

smiled at the Portuguese nurse as he ushered Jane towards the main door. 'Sorry to rush you away, you were obviously enjoying your chat, but it's too fine a day to spend indoors and we are supposed to be on holiday, not wasting time in clinics.'

CHAPTER TEN

'ARE we pleased to see you.' Anne Golding, hair escaping from her usually neat ponytail, beamed as Jane walked into the nurses' changing-room. 'I thought nine o'clock was never going to get here. Did you have a good holiday, by the way?' She studied Jane, her head to one side. 'You look as though you did.'

'Yes, marvellous. I won't bore you with all the details now, though. I gather you've been very busy?' Taking her brush from her bag, Jane pulled vigorously at her hair, now softened into a longer bob about her face.

'It's been murder,' Anne sighed.

Quickly smoothing on some lip gloss, Jane pulled at the waistband of her uniform dress, and with her bag in hand followed the other nurse to the office.

Anne was right; Jane frowned as she wrote details of the day's happenings in her small notebook. Where was the peace and calm of the week before she went away? She rolled her eyes as she glanced again through her notes.

'Let's hope the night is a bit quieter. Two admissions, one cardiac arrest, one failed pacemaker in one day.' Jane gulped, chewing anxiously at her bottom lip as she walked into the small ward of six patients. 'More than enough to be going on with.'

'I'm glad you're familiar with Coronary Care,'

Jane muttered gratefully to the other nurse. 'I feel as though I've forgotten all I ever knew.' She was silent as she sorted the charts and collected syringes for the drugs to be given. Despite her attempts at concentrating on her work, her thoughts would drift back to Oporto. Their day out had started so well. After the visit to the clinic, they'd driven up through the zig-zag contours of the Douro valley, the stark granite outlines of the rocky surfaces at times reminding her of Cornwall.

Their lunch in a small *pousada*, its blue-tiled walls and wooden furniture a setting made for romance, had been all she could have hoped for. And several times, Matthew had looked at her with such yearning, she'd trembled inside. He must be going to say something, she'd thought.

But they'd been interrupted halfway through the meal by old friends of Matthew's who had greeted him with cries of surprise and delight. Any chance of quiet conversation had gone, lost in the general hubbub as the other couple joined them. Had Matthew intended to discuss anything further? She would probably never know. His cool friendliness had made the remaining two days of the holiday a pleasant experience but in no way special as she'd hoped.

'If you like, I'll go round and settle the patients,' a cheerful Marie suggested, pulling Jane's thoughts abruptly back to the present. 'You see to the medication.'

Jane nodded her agreement. Flicking open the treatment cards, she listed the drugs, then walked from bed to bed, checking details as she did so. The monitors flashed reassuringly and everything seemed under control.

Ernest Brown, the patient who'd suffered the cardiac arrest during the afternoon, still looked very shocked, hunched in the bed in the corner, his face a sickly grey under the bright fluorescent lights. As Jane pushed back the edge of the curtain, her first sight was of a familiar broad-shouldered figure bending over the bed.

She felt such warmth, such delight at seeing him, she was surprised that Matthew couldn't sense it, but he didn't seem to notice her arrival; his attention was firmly fixed on his patient, his eyes gazing upwards as he listened carefully through the stethoscope to Mr Brown's heart.

Jane smiled at the man who lay back against his pillows, trying to disguise her dismay at the waxy appearance of his skin.

He looks awful, she thought, and glanced at the monitor in an effort to assess what had happened. But the abnormalities were different from those she'd seen in the past.

I must get Matthew to explain it to me, if he has time, she worried. As though he'd read her thoughts, he glanced up with a reassuring smile, folding his stethoscope neatly and placing it in the pocket of his white coat.

'As you can probably see,' he pointed to the monitor above the bed, 'Mr Brown is having rather a lot of coupled beats. When you have a minute, could you do a repeat ECG for me?' He turned back to the patient. 'Nothing to worry about, Mr Brown,

it just means the heartbeats doubling up a bit. I want
to try and find out why.'

'Here we are.' The ECG machine was as contrary
as a supermarket trolley and Jane swore softly under
her breath as she struggled it into place. She glanced
up to see doctor and patient smiling sympathetically
at her efforts.

'Sorry about the language,' she muttered red-
faced. 'I'm not the world's best driver.'

'You're doing OK, Nurse,' Mr Brown reassured
her.

'Call me Jane, please.' She held the leads aloft. 'I
expect you've had this done plenty of times before,
haven't you?'

He nodded, and with a small sigh unbuttoned his
striped pyjama jacket.

Carefully, Jane attached the leads in position and
watched fascinated as the machine spewed out first
of all the reading in a frantic zig-zag dance then
rattled out a suggested diagnosis.

'Don't know why we need doctors,' she confided
as she cleared everything away. 'These machines not
only record what's wrong, but write it out as well.'

'I'd hate to think we were expendable.'

Jane swung round at the teasing note in Matthew's
voice.

'I didn't for a moment suggest such a thing,' she
grinned in answer. 'But you have to admit that it is
pretty unnerving!' She pointed to the corner of the
paper. 'It even tells you what's wrong.'

'Yes, but notice the final comment,' Matthew said
quickly. ' "Please refer for medical opinion." At least
the machine knows we're still needed.'

'Don't say anything about machines "knowing",' Jane shuddered. 'The mere idea gives me the creeps.' Swiftly, she helped Mr Brown to fasten his pyjama top, and pulled the duvet with its cheery yellow cover into place. Soft-footed, Matthew moved to the desk, the ECG graph in his hand.

'Have you got any pain at the moment, Ernest? You don't mind if I call you by your first name, do you?'

Her patient shook his head. 'No, on both counts. I'm feeling much more comfortable than earlier, thanks.'

Jane glanced once again at the monitor. Matthew had been quite right, she thought, when he'd said that it was reassuring to have the monitor show exactly what was happening. And her patient certainly wasn't being treated in an impersonal way, despite everyone's reliance on machines.

She went to the nurse's station but Matthew had disappeared. Surely he hadn't left the unit without at least saying where he was going?

'Have you seen Dr Carvalho?' Jane turned as Marie appeared with a tray of hot drinks.

'I think he went to the path lab with some blood samples.' Marie rested the tray on the table at the end of the first bed and passed a mug of hot milk to the elderly woman, who barely glanced up from her newspaper to take the drink.

'He's coming back, though, isn't he?' Jane muttered anxiously. Her earlier confidence that all seemed well had gone. Now every patient's condition seemed unstable, putting her in the middle of some bizarre dance, turning nervously from one

monitor to the next. A bit like the game of 'What's
the time, Mr Wolf?' she thought, giggling to herself
at the idea of the monitors changing as she looked
away, to try and catch her out; just as she and her
friends used to creep up behind 'Mr Wolf' all those
years ago at school.

With a sigh, she carried on with the drugs; digoxin
for one to regulate the heartbeat, propanol for
another patient, making sure that an infusion with
potassium was running correctly.

'I've finished the drinks; do you want a hand?'
Marie's cheery face appeared around the screen,
glancing at Jane by Mr Brown's bedside. Both nurses
went hurriedly to the desk.

'He looks terrible,' Marie said softly.

'I know. I'm sure he feels much worse than he
says.' Jane looked across the unit. 'You can smell
that acrid smell of fear and his skin is so clammy.'
Quickly she riffled through the paperwork and pro-
duced the ECG reading she'd taken earlier.

'Take a look at that.'

Softly Marie whistled through her teeth.

'I should bleep Matthew Carvalho.'

'I think he's already seen this,' Jane protested. 'I
don't want to give him the impression that I'm
panicking.' She could just imagine Matthew, an
expression of slight surprise on those dark features,
that she'd called him because she couldn't cope. It
would put paid to her frequent protestations of being
independent. Even while on holiday, she'd been
unable to prevent herself showing how well she
could manage. Still, the welfare of her patient was
far more important than any false sense of pride.

'I think that's one very dicky heart and Ernest himself looks worse by the minute,' Marie muttered.

'Right, you've convinced me.'

But as Jane picked up the telephone, any doubts about what she should do were pushed aside. With a gurgling noise that broke into the nurses' discussion, Mr Brown slipped sideways from his pillow.

Quickly Jane, closely followed by Marie, whirled into the cubicle, her heart thudding at the sight of the intermittent line on the monitor.

'Oh, no, not on my first night back from holiday,' she groaned as she wound the bed flat and gently straightened Mr Brown.

'Cardiac arrest,' she muttered through clenched teeth; Marie quickly pressed the arrest call button before hurrying back to Jane's side.

'What's the routine here?' Gasping with effort, Jane had started cardiac massage, resting one knee on the edge of the bed to give herself more leverage. Marie swiftly placed a mask over the airway she'd placed in Ernest's mouth and began to inflate his lungs with a black rebreathing bag.

'Come on,' Jane groaned as she pumped steadily at the man's ribcage.

Sweat was already pouring down her face and back when suddenly the curtains were swished open. Jane thought she'd never seen a more welcome sight than that of Matthew's broad figure, followed closely by the anaesthetist on call.

'Given any drugs?'

Matthew snapped out the words as the anaesthetist opened his emergency bag and pulled out laryngoscope and a tube, ready to pass it into the patient's trachea.

'No. We've just been hand ventilating and doing cardiac massage,' Jane muttered breathlessly.

'Well done; get me adrenalin, one in ten thousand, and an ampoule of atropine.'

He glanced at the monitor screen once more, which now showed an occasional wave as Jane continued to press down on the patient's chest.

Swiftly, Matthew took the syringe from Marie and shot the contents into the drip, watching the screen intently.

'Do you want me to intubate?' The anaesthetist paused at the head of the bed.

'Better, I think. We're getting some rhythm but it might be as well to have him ventilated overnight. Let's try another adrenalin.' Matthew refilled the syringe and once again fed the contents into the infusion line.

Talk about teamwork, Jane thought a short time later, a trifle smugly, she knew, but there was an enormous satisfaction in seeing the results of their efforts. She stretched her aching arms and shoulders.

'I feel as though I've been working for hours,' she observed. She was amazed to see that barely half an hour had passed since the first alarm on the monitor. Ernest lay peacefully on the bed, his breathing regular, his heartbeat moving along evenly, and at a steady rate.

'Phew, it's lucky you girls were so on the ball.' Matthew gathered the bits and pieces scattered everywhere and placed them neatly on a bedside trolley.

'His skin's pinking up nicely,' the anaesthetist observed, looking intently at Mr Brown's ears and fingers.

'Yes, we seem to have got him back. Well done, you two.' He smiled and patted each nurse on the arm before picking up the blood result forms which had been scattered over the floor in the general turmoil.

'I hope that isn't going to happen too often,' Jane whispered to Marie as they returned to the nurses' station.

'I'm going to put the kettle on,' Marie muttered and Jane nodded her heartfelt agreement. She felt as though she'd been put through a wringer, her hair clinging damply to her forehead, her uniform stuck to the full length of her spine.

'Tired, Jane?' Matthew smiled sympathetically. 'It's really tough, doing exernal cardiac massage, isn't it? Especially when you're not very tall.'

'I'm not that small.' She grinned to take the sting from her words. 'Anyway, they say good things come in little parcels,' she added, wincing at the cliché as soon as she spoke. Tense though she was, she was shocked when her joking remark fell so flat, for Matthew frowned heavily, his eyes darkening to look almost black in the light that shone from the lamp on the desk.

'Jane, for goodness' sake.' His sigh expressed his exasperation as no words would have done. 'I thought you'd got over all that touchiness.'

'I wasn't being touchy,' Jane stammered, her green eyes wide as she stared into the depths of

Matthew's dark blue gaze. She wasn't sure if he was joking or not.

'I can't believe that you still take offence, after all this time. . .' He broke off abruptly, as Marie reappeared, carrying a tray of coffee. 'Mmm, that smells good.' His smile at Marie contrasted strongly with the way he'd looked at Jane moments ago. Don't say one silly little remark is enough to spoil things between us, Jane fretted.

Though she'd been disappointed that he'd said nothing more about their relationship since their time in Portugal, he'd still treated her with such consideration, at times she'd dared to hope. But for what? My idea that Matthew was about to express undying devotion at the restaurant must have been no more than wishful thinking, she thought wryly. I should just thank my lucky stars he's not discovered how I feel about him.

'Sorry if I upset you,' she muttered, shamefaced. But her apology fell as flat as her earlier remark.

'They look very tempting,' Jane said in hearty tones, staring at the cakes on the tray as Marie appeared. 'And there's nothing to beat the smell of coffee, is there?' She inhaled dramatically.

'It's only instant,' Marie apologised, surprise on her face at Jane's apparent enthusiasm. 'Sugar, Matthew?'

'No, thanks. Just black for me.'

'Sweet enough, eh?' Marie grinned as she poured.

He glanced up from the notes spread on the desk where he'd been scribbling steadily since the emergency. 'It does seem to be cliché night, doesn't it?' Picking up his cup, he walked swiftly from the desk to the bedside, leaving a pair of open-mouthed nurses gazing after him.

'He was a bit off,' Marie frowned. 'What have you done to upset him?'

'Don't know,' Jane shrugged as though she didn't care what Matthew said or did. But she did care, oh, how she cared. The idea that their lives would one day go in different directions was almost too painful to contemplate.

'But I thought you were good friends.' Marie stirred busily at her mug. 'Haven't you just been on holiday together?'

'It wasn't quite like that,' Jane corrected hastily. 'I stayed with his cousin in Portugal and Matthew joined us there for a few days.'

'Oh, well, probably just a lovers' tiff. He'll soon come round.'

'There's nothing like that between us, I can assure you,' Jane said drily. 'Anyway, enough of my stupid problems. I'll drink this, then check that Mr Brown is OK.'

'It's all right, I can see his monitor easily from here. We'll soon know if there is anything wrong. You did reset the alarms, didn't you?'

'Of course.' Jane slumped into the chair and sipped at her coffee. 'I'd forgotten how tiring cardiac massage is,' she said quietly. 'I feel as though my neck has been twisted like a corkscrew. Probably the combination of physical and mental tension. Ohh!' She'd just put her cup on the tray when strong warm fingers began to dig gently into the aching muscles of her shoulders.

'Lean your head forward,' Matthew ordered, 'and I'll see if I can ease some of that stiffness for you.'

'I wasn't actually asking. . .' Jane began, her voice muffled as she gazed obediently towards the floor.

'Just be quiet and for once do as you're told without arguing.'

'Yes, sir!' she muttered defiantly under her breath. But she had to admit to herself after a few moments that the touch of Matthew's hands worked like magic, as he seemed instinctively to know exactly where to reach the worst of her aching muscles.

I could stay like this forever, she thought, each supple movement of Matthew's fingers releasing her tension. His hands smelt of soap and a mild antiseptic but even that wasn't enough to take away the strongly sensual nature of his caresses.

Still with her eyes closed, she slowly raised her head and turned it to one side. But she was drawn abruptly from her dreamy state as he gently smoothed the soft skin of her cheek. Hastily, Jane opened her eyes, realising with a surge of embarrassment that all had gone quiet.

To her intense relief, Marie was at the bedside talking to the anaesthetist, and, as far as Jane could tell, neither had noticed her response to Matthew's touch.

He bent forward and pressed his face close to her. 'Better now?' he whispered.

'I'm fine.' Blinking as though she'd woken from a deep sleep, Jane stood and moved round behind the desk.

'What's the matter?' Matthew's eyes glinted mischievously. His shirt collar was askew, ruckled over the corner of his white coat, and she had to clasp her hands together to stop them reaching out to straighten his collar for him.

'My aches and pains have gone, thank you,' she muttered, rubbing her hand against the back of her neck, as though she could resurrect the sensation of Matthew's touch by doing so.

'I didn't exactly mean that,' he murmured. 'Jane, I seem to be repeating myself, but I must talk to you. You must realise that I just want to take care, not take over.' His earlier bad mood had gone and there was a yearning note in his voice that sent Jane nervously to Mr Brown's bedside before Matthew could say any more. She was scared—yes, scared by the gravity of his tone.

Goodness knew what sort of impression she'd given him, almost swooning at his touch; many more minutes and she could have swooned into his arms. She bit her lip, forcing back a giggle at the old-fashioned phrase and the bizarre picture it conjured up.

She was relieved to see that Ernest was breathing normally, the black bag inflating and collapsing steadily. As Jane got to the bedside, the anaesthetist removed the tube and placed an oxygen mask over Mr Brown's nose and chin.

'Could you help me to sit him up, please?' Carefully Jane avoided looking at Matthew as he went silently to the far side of the bed, and gently placed one arm around the patient's shoulders. Pressing the lever, Jane lifted the back of the bed and settled a very bewildered Mr Brown comfortably against the pillows.

'It's all right, I can manage now, thank you.' Jane gathered up the debris, the syringes and ampoules all placed tidily in a receiver, the spare tubes and tapes back in the resuscitation box.

'Did you see that ECG I did just before Mr Brown collapsed?' she called over her shoulder.

But Matthew didn't seem to hear as he picked up his briefcase and went to the office with the anaesthetist, closing the door firmly behind him.

'Oh, don't talk to me, then.' Jane shrugged. Feeling almost bereft because Matthew had gone, she turned with what she hoped was a reassuring smile to a very drowsy Ernest Brown.

The next hour flew by as the nurses settled the other patients, who were keyed up to an extra level of nervousness by the emergency. Jane was kept busy with sedation, hot drinks and reassuring chats before she and Marie were able to get the last patient settled and could lower the lights; except for the dim lamp at the desk and a small extra light by Ernest as he gradually dozed, his restlessness a worry every time he moved.

'Have you known Dr Carvalho long?' Marie sat heavily in one of the upright chairs in the middle of the unit, and leaned back, speaking quietly above the muted sounds, an occasional groan, someone's gentle snore and the steady blip-blip from a monitor.

'No, only since I came to work here.' Jane blinked at the question as she rested her arms on the desk. 'Why?'

'Oh, I got the impression that you'd been friends for ages. You seem to get on so well.'

'Perhaps, but it wasn't always like that.' Jane giggled, the relief from the earlier tension making her a little light-headed. 'In fact the first time we met,' she said softly, 'we nearly had a stand-up fight. He accused me of tampering with his car and got really shirty, I can tell you.'

'And had you?'

'Well, not exactly. But I must admit I gave the wretched thing a good big thump. He'd parked right in front of my car so that I couldn't move and I was in a such a hurry. . . What's the matter?' For Marie was grimacing and staring over Jane's shoulder at the office door. As if from a distance, Jane heard the dull click of its closing. She didn't dare to look behind her, but the force of Matthew's gaze boring into her back seemed to generate its own heat. She waited for his comments, scarcely able to draw breath. I hope he didn't hear me, she prayed silently, crossing her fingers in an agony of embarrassment.

But she wasn't to learn if he'd heard her or not.

'I forgot to tell you earlier,' he said coolly. 'Cliff Jennings went to Theatre yesterday and had a coronary artery bypass graft. It was in the nature of an emergency so I was unable to arrange for you to go and watch.'

'Is he all right?'

'I believe he's doing very well.' Matthew nodded reassuringly. 'Has already been extubated, and taken off the ventilator. His wife is delighted.'

'That's marvellous. I must try and visit him, when he's a bit better.'

'I'll see if I can arrange for you to see a cardiac operation some time when it's not so busy.'

'If it's not too much trouble?'

'No trouble. If you need me tonight, buzz me directly, especially if Mr Brown shows any sign of deterioration.' He strolled from the ward, talking animatedly to his companion.

Jane couldn't control a despondent sigh as Matthew left. It probably sounded as though she was making fun when she spoke to Marie about the episode with his car. And he'd been so calm and reassuring during the time of the cardiac arrest, then taken the trouble to massage her neck. In fact, she'd wondered if he was about to say something, something important. Still, the middle of the coronary care unit wasn't exactly the place for a heart-to-heart — she smiled at the unconscious pun — it wasn't surprising that nothing had developed.

'Me and my big mouth,' she muttered under her breath, pretending not to see the curious look Marie gave her as they went back to work.

But she didn't have time to worry about Matthew during the hours that followed, for Ernest's condition was so unstable that both nurses were kept at full stretch and twice Matthew was called back to the ward. On each occasion he was polite and professional, with never a hint of anything warmer in his tone.

She had never been more pleased to hear the early morning chorus from the birds in the oak trees at the edge of the hospital grounds, nor to see the daylight lighting up the windows.

Giving out the morning drugs, taking blood for

routine tests and making sure that all the X-ray request forms were completed made the last hour of duty a tiring final canter for both herself and Marie.

'As you said so plainly yesterday evening,' Jane grinned to the early day shift, 'thank God you're here.'

'Been a long night, has it?'

Jane nodded wearily and handed over the report as quickly as her tired brain would allow.

'Mr Brown's wife is coming in at about nine. They live quite a long way away and she doesn't drive herself, so she was a bit anxious at the idea of dragging out a neighbour in the early hours of the morning.'

'I don't think I could sit at home when my husband was that poorly, could you?' Anne Golding grimaced as she noted the details, giving Jane a farewell pat on the back. Jane waved in answer, calling 'Goodbye' to Marie as she hurried through the swing doors and went to the lift.

What a night! she thought as she waited for the lift to arrive. And it wasn't helped by all the business with Matthew. First of all he takes offence, then he starts to massage my neck, sending me into ecstasies — she shivered at the memory — after that. . . Jane shrugged as the lift drew up in front of her then couldn't control a blush as the object of her thoughts was revealed by the opening of the doors.

'Good morning, Jane.' He looked as fresh and as clean as though he'd just come from the shower. Perhaps he has, Jane thought, looking at his slicked-back hair, seal-dark in the corridor lights. Just as though he hadn't been called out several times during the night. His blue shirt and dark red tie contrasted with the crispness of his white coat and there was a drift of cologne as Jane moved past him.

Her brief, 'Good morning,' sounded abrupt, even to her own ears.

'Jane, I'm glad I've seen you. We need to talk. And I'm not allowing anything to stand in my way this time.' He thrust out a determined foot to stop the lift door closing and gazed intently at her.

'What is there. . .?'

'Not here.' He seized her arm and pulled her back from the lift. 'Are you too tired to go somewhere for breakfast?'

'I'm afraid I am more than ready for my bed. Anyway, I have to get home for Mum and the children.'

'Now, don't jump to the wrong conclusions if I tell you that I spoke to your Mother last night and if you want. . .'

'You rang Mum? Why didn't you say something?' Her heart started beating rapidly as she reached out and seized Matthew's arm. 'There's nothing wrong, is there?'

'Of course there's nothing wrong.' He spoke so loudly that a cleaner busy with mop and bucket at the far end of the corridor stopped with his mop at full stretch and stared curiously at them both.

'I warned her that you might be a bit late getting home, that's all. Oh, for goodness' sake, don't look at me with those big green eyes all soulful, as though I've gone mad. Come with me.' Not waiting for any discussion, Matthew took her hand and towed her behind him. 'In there.' None too gently, he pushed her ahead of him into a large linen cupboard and closed the door behind them.

'Sit down.' Her face a picture of bewilderment, Jane perched obediently on the edge of a shelf.

'Matthew, I. . . Ooh.' She was rendered speechless as, without warning, he leaned forward and kissed her, a full, powerful kiss on the mouth.

'Jane, I promise you I haven't gone completely insane, but I shall do, if I don't get the chance to ask you something.'

'I'm sorry, but I don't know. . .' She frowned up at him.

'Oh, come here.' Groaning deep in his throat, Matthew pulled her to him and kissed her once more. But this kiss was different. It started as a gentle butterfly touch at the corner of her mouth then feathered slowly across her lips, setting a trail of electric sensation in the delicate skin.

'Matthew, what are you doing?' She pulled back and gazed at his face, inches from her.

'What do you think I'm doing?' His laughter was husky as he kissed her again, the pressure of his mouth matched by the fervour with which Jane responded. Oblivous of their surroundings, her eyes closed, she felt she was drowning in the sweetness of his embrace, pressing herself to him, conscious of the strength of his arms and the powerful breadth of his chest as he held her near.

Reeling slightly as Matthew suddenly released her, she stared at him, her green eyes wide, her breathing rapid. She was astonished to see that Matthew looked as disturbed as she felt.

'Matthew. . .' she began.

'You must think I've taken leave of my senses.'
He laughed softly and cupped her face in his hands.
'I've been trying to get you to myself ever since that
day in Oporto, but there has always been someone
or something to interrupt us, before I had a chance
to say. . .' He paused and for a moment looked
almost shy.

'Say what?' Jane whispered, hardly daring to
believe her suspicions.

'Oh, you must have guessed, surely? You must
have some idea how I feel about you.'

'No.' A mischievous glint in her eye, Jane shook
her head.

'Perhaps this will give you some idea.' Once more
he kissed her, his mouth moving softly across her
face and down to the throbbing pulse of her neck.
'I'm trying to tell you that I love you and I want to
marry you,' he murmured against the soft skin
beneath her ear.

'Oh.'

'Is that all you can say, "Oh"?'

'Oh, yes, please.' Jane swallowed.

'You mean you will?' He straightened and stared
at her disbelievingly.

'You idiot,' she said softly, 'did you seriously
think I wouldn't accept?'

'Well, I was sure you couldn't love me as I love
you, but I did hope that there might be some
tenderness, some feeling that would grow with time.'

'I've loved you for long ages, as Emma would
say.' She smiled tenderly. It was a change for her to
feel the stronger, to realise that Matthew needed
reassurance. She paused and drew back in dismay as

a thought struck her. 'I can't marry you. What about Emma and Harry?'

'What about them? Of course they're included in our future.' He shook her gently. 'Did you honestly think that I would expect you to forget about them?'

'But it's not very fair that you should. . .'

'Rubbish. They might not be your children but they are part of you and as such I would never consider not taking them on.'

He bent and kissed her again. 'Not the most romantic setting, is it?' He grinned and gestured at the shelves surrounding them. 'But I'll make it up to you, I promise.'

'Oi, what's going on in there?' Even the impatient knocking at the door and the irate voice couldn't spoil Jane's happiness.

'We'd better go,' she giggled.

'Oh, Jane, I could stay here forever. I love your smile, your gutsiness, even your quick answers. Now, kiss me once more before we leave,' Matthew murmured. 'I still can't believe it's true that. . .' He blinked and shook his head, holding her close. 'My darling, darling little. . .'

'Not so much of the "little",' Jane frowned.

'Little, small, *petite*, tiny, diminutive,' he teased, 'just perfect in every way, "Just Jane".'

SUMMER SPECIAL!

Four exciting new Romances for the price of three

Each Romance features British heroines and their encounters with dark and desirable Mediterranean men. *Plus, a free Elmlea recipe booklet inside every pack.*

So sit back and enjoy your sumptuous summer reading pack and indulge yourself with the free Elmlea recipe ideas.

Available July 1994   Price £5.70

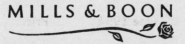

MILLS & BOON

MILLS & BOON

Proudly present...

CHARLOTTE LAMB'S
♥ *100th* ♥
ROMANCE

This is a remarkable achievement for a writer who had her first Mills & Boon novel published in 1973. Some six million words later and with sales around the world, her novels continue to be popular with romance fans everywhere.

Her centenary romance **'VAMPIRE LOVER'** is a suspense-filled story of dark desires and tangled emotions—Charlotte Lamb at her very best.

Published: June 1994   **Price:** £1.90

Available from WH Smith, John Menzies, Volume One, Forbuoys, Martins, Woolworths, Tesco, Asda, Safeway and other paperback stockists.
Also available from Mills & Boon Reader Service, FREEPOST, PO Box 236, Croydon, Surrey CR9 9EL (UK Postage & Packing free).

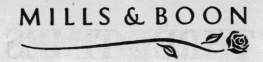

MILLS & BOON

LOVE ON CALL

The books for enjoyment this month are:

TROUBLED HEARTS Christine Adams
SUNLIGHT AND SHADOW Frances Crowne
PARTNERS IN PRIDE Drusilla Douglas
A TESTING TIME Meredith Webber

♥　♥　♥　♥　♥

Treats in store!

Watch next month for the following absorbing stories:

HEARTS OUT OF TIME Judith Ansell
THE DOCTOR'S DAUGHTER Margaret Barker
MIDNIGHT SUN Rebecca Lang
ONE CARING HEART Marion Lennox

LOVE ON CALL
4 FREE BOOKS AND 2 FREE GIFTS
FROM MILLS & BOON

Capture all the drama and emotion of a hectic medical world when you accept 4 Love on Call romances PLUS a cuddly teddy bear and a mystery gift - absolutely FREE and without obligation. And, if you choose, go on to enjoy 4 exciting Love on Call romances every month for only £1.80 each! Be sure to return the coupon below today to: Mills & Boon Reader Service, FREEPOST, PO Box 236, Croydon, Surrey CR9 9EL.

✂ — — — — — — [**NO STAMP REQUIRED**] — — — — —

YES! Please rush me 4 FREE Love on Call books and 2 FREE gifts! Please also reserve me a Reader Service subscription, which means I can look forward to receiving 4 brand new Love on Call books for only £7.20 every month, postage and packing FREE. If I choose not to subscribe, I shall write to you within 10 days and still keep my FREE books and gifts. I may cancel or suspend my subscription at any time. I am over 18 years. Please write in BLOCK CAPITALS.

Ms/Mrs/Miss/Mr _____ **EP63D**

Address _____

_____

Postcode _____ Signature _____